The Angel
and
The Boatman

An Unusual Love Story
yet in the face of death, anything is possible

Paula F. Howard

Copyright Page

Written by Paula F. Howard
Cover Design by Paula F. Howard

PRINTED IN THE UNITED STATES OF AMERICA
A HOWARD ACTIVITY PRESS
First Edition: September, 2019
Second Edition: May, 2021

ISBN: 9781689985345

More copies may be ordered online at Amazon.com

or through

https://www.TheWritersMall.com

Table of Contents

Dedication   5

The Santa   7

Discovered   11

Big Trouble   14

How It all Happened   17

Other Ideas   22

Breaking Out   24

Crash Landing   27

Finding the Baby   31

The Aging   33

Marcy   36

Becoming the Boatman   39

The Golden Ticket   44

Where is Everybody? 47

Abducted!   50

Angel's Choice   54

Table of Contents continued...

In the Bardo   57

The Agreement   60

Meanwhile . . . in Hell   64

The Escape   68

Angel in Hell   74

The Super Power   76

Passing Years 80

The Rescue (Again)   84

Into the Future 88

The Message   92

Meet the Author   94

Excerpt from "The Hidden Pricetag" 95

Dedication

To my mom and dad who raised me with love.

To my children whom I raised with love.

To my husband who I live with in love.

To my sisters, grandchildren, son-in-law and

especially, my brother-in-law who told me about

the Hacker,

I send you love.

(Hmmm. Love, love, love...there's a theme going on.)

The Santa

The tiny elf watched Santa Claus and smiled a crooked smile.

It's good he doesn't know who he really is. He wouldn't like it very much, the tiny man thought.

A long line of children were waiting to get onto Santa's lap. Some were fidgeting, some were crying, only one little boy was staring straight ahead.

Hmm, he's a strange one. Wonder what he's thinking.

The little boy wasn't thinking at all. He was calculating, figuring out the square quadrants and time it would take to make it to the moon. He planned to hide out there…on the moon. Until he could be picked up by The Boatman. They were going to "rendezvous."

Santa, meanwhile, was laughing and talking to the little girl on his knee, the one with a pretty smile. She was telling him what she wanted for Christmas.

The elf looked at a special recorder on the ground behind Santa's chair. It was recording everything, not just for parents, but…for the "Operation".

Santa was a plant. He was a front. He was a fraud. Only…bless his soul, he had no clue.

"…And if you're good, Santa will bring you a present," the big man was saying, his white beard a stark contrast against a red suit, "But, if you're naughty, you'll get a piece of coal."

Hmm, I wonder if being Santa exonerates him from his 'dishonorable deed.' Obviously, he doesn't realize how serious it is to be recording children's thoughts for the store's profit. He simply doesn't realize the serious nature of collecting a child's words and deeds, the elf thought.

The recordings weren't going to be replayed just so parents knew what to buy. No. All recordings were going to be stored – forever – in the Computer of the Universe, known as Life's Database, the Akashic Records, or just plain Man's Memory. These recordings were used to recall a person's life at their time of death. Nothing was ever forgotten.

The Elf jumped off the platform and shook his head.

Geez, I should have paid more attention in class. The one that taught the difference between thinking, saying or doing something. He stopped for a moment and thought back to his school days.

If I'd just remembered that intentions are as strong as actions for racking up future obligations, I wouldn't have gotten that question wrong on my final exam.

What most people don't realize is that whatever they think about with strong feeling, begins shaping their future. He laughed and started walking again.

That's how the world works. But hardly anybody knows it, the Elf thought. It's all about 'karma'.

Getting that particular question wrong on his exam about thoughts as well as actions creating a person's future had made him miss a perfect score. He'd never forgotten it.

But, he had paid strict attention in "Future Positions Available" class. It had been his favorite. That's because his true intentions were to become a boatman. It was an honor and privilege to anyone aspiring to upper celestial management.

A boatman's position was to travel the Universe collecting souls and carrying them over the River Styx. That was just a metaphor. The river wasn't actually a water river. It was a line of demarcation between this Life and the Next, or the next level of Living that every soul reaches.

No one knew how many dimensions there really were. Life just kept going on and on ad infinitum until one reached Perfection. But a boatman's job was the highest level possible for his pay grade and the Elf meant to get there. He meant to have a boatman's job.

Oh, yes indeed!

"I don't wanna!" cried out a little kid. He was fighting the mother, not wanting to get onto Santa's knee.

"Jeffrey! Stop that! You know Santa just wants to talk to you." The woman was large, her hat askew on top of her hair which was sticking out all over. "Just tell Santa what you want for Christmas!" she clearly didn't know herself, and she needed to know.

"Ho, ho, ho," remarked Santa, reaching for Jeffrey.

 "No! You can't make me!" The little boy kicked Santa in the shin and ran off the platform.

The Elf looked at the recorder. It was recording Jeffrey's tantrum.

"Uh, oh, karma," the Elf said. "He'll pay for that."

In fact, the machine was still recording everything, not just Jeffrey's tantrum but every thought, word and deed in the stratosphere.

That's how Santa supposedly knew if someone had been 'naughty' or 'nice'. The Elf laughed to himself. *It's all in the Database, waiting for future review at someone's passing.*

But Santa wasn't the only one interested in the recordings, Upper Celestial Management wanted to know about thoughts and intentions, too, so they could eventually schedule the Boatman.

"That's why, I'll be a boatman one day," the Elf said aloud. "Then, I'll know Life's secrets, too."

He was completely aware that his intentions were beginning to shape his future, and smiled.

1

Discovered

The old man bent over a crooked cane that clacked as he walked in a stumbling fashion. Reaching the grocery store, he entered, and made his way slowly to the fresh produce section.

His gait was awkward: cane, shuffle, cane, shuffle. Stopping in front of the ripe, red tomatoes, he reached for a plump one. Feeling it, he put it down and reached for another. The fruits were both hard against his fingers. Only this one gave slightly under his pinch. He raised it to his nose and briefly inhaled. No smell.

"Bahh, what's the use! They don't make 'em like they used to. No smell, no good." He put it down and shifted his weight from the cane, leaning against the stall.

A grocery cart approached from his far left. The back of a small head was barely visible above a baby seat nestled inside the cart. Blonde tufts of hair were sticking upward, slightly waving in the air. A young, pleasant-looking woman was pushing the cart and baby down the aisle. Every now and then she would smile down at the hidden face and coo at the tiny human.

Something familiar caught the old man's gaze. He couldn't quite put a finger on it, but...something. The old man watched as the cart wheeled slowly toward him… closer, almost even with him as he leaned against the tomato bin.

Then, when it was directly across from the old man, the baby's small head bobbled a little. The head sat on top of a not quite-strong little neck. Suddenly, a movement made the baby look over at the old man.

Their eyes connected.

The little one looked directly into the withered old face ....and smiled. His gaze held steady and straight.

"Aaaaggghhhhh!" the old man cried out. Losing his balance and falling backwards into the tomato bin, he knocked a number of them. Tomatoes rolled off the bin, hit the ground, and scattered like a bunch of children playing tag. They were everywhere in a matter of seconds.

The old man caught his balance, then hobbled as quickly as possible toward the exit.

It's him! he screamed inwardly. *I don't know how, but he's HERE!*

Meanwhile, the baby looked up into his mother's face and smiled. His eyes held a knowing far beyond his tender age.

Breathless, the old man reached his ramshackle home. Pushing open the door, he entered just as his legs buckled beneath him. Catching the arm of an old, leather lounge chair, he threw himself into the seat. The cane clattered to the floor. He was sweating profusely now. Water rivulets snaked down his neck into his tattered shirt. A body odor began rising into the air.

How can he be here? I was so careful this time! I can't be seen again!

He reached for the phone, an old landline, and dialed a number

"H'llo?" the voice was low, raspy, unconcerned.

"He's here! I saw him at the market. He's little yet, but that won't be for long!"

"'Ow can you be sure? You've been wrong before."

"I will never forget those eyes! Don't matter whose body they're in! It's Him, I tell you, it's HIM!"

"All right. Stay calm, I'll get the word out. Stay home! And don't go by the windows!"

Hanging up, the old man slouched deep into its cushions. It felt good to be home. Safe. In his hideout. It had been years since he had felt this afraid. He managed to be unseen for such a long time. Even his neighbors barely knew him. He liked it that way.

***

The young mother reached her car with the baby and groceries. She opened the rear door. Then, smoothly lifting the baby out of the grocery cart, she placed him into a car seat and buckled him in. The baby's eyes stared blankly ahead.

Inside the baby's head the Invader was thinking: These tiny bodies are so compact.

He adjusted his vision through the eye sockets.

This kid might be a good one, though, I can feel his abilities even in one so small. I might put a tag on him and see what he's like in a few earth years.

The Invader reset the baby's inner time clock to wake in an hour. That would allow him time to leave the body and go explore. He would try to see where the Grimlot had gone.

Spotting him in the grocery store by the tomato bin had been a surprise. There was no mistaking that odor, though, even mixed with the smells of an old earth man. No mistaking that odor at all.

The Invader slipped out of the baby's right eye socket and was gone.

As the mother pulled her car out of the parking spot, she glanced in the rearview mirror. The baby was already asleep.

That was quick, she noted to herself. The baby's head leaned back against the car seat. All seemed normal. But it wasn't. It wasn't at all.

2

Big Trouble

The Grimlot had been here a long time.

He had not come to earth as an old man, but as a baby, just like the one who had terrified him in the supermarket.

The one that looked like a baby, but he knew was not.

Waiting for the phone to ring was nerve-wracking. Such an antiquated method of communication. Where he came from, messages traveled at the speed of thought.

Not here, though, not on this planet. But that's what probably saved him after all these eons.

Being in the Witness Protection Program for his kind, meant adjusting to all sorts of inconveniences. The least of which was talking over contraptions that were centuries behind modes of communication like on his home planet, Orieste, in the galaxy MACS-0647-JD.

Even that wasn't his real home, just the boatmen where he had entered this Universe. Orieste was far from Earth, some 13.3 billion light years away to be exact. The oldest planet known in this Universe.

He had crisscrossed so many time zones and planets, had so many identities even he couldn't remember his own trail.

No, his real home wasn't on this planet, nor in this constellation. It wasn't even on this plane of existence.

He was very, very far from home.

His Witness Protection identity had been so well contrived, in fact, it seemed impossible for the Boatman to have found him.

But he had.

The Boatman was here. The Grimlot recognized that gaze no matter what kind of body he was wearing. No matter what shape or form he controlled.

The first question was: How had he done it? Secondly: Where could the Grimlot hide now?

It was far too close to The Trial for any mistakes to happen. He couldn't be taken by The Boatman…at any cost!

His hidden identity had taken 50 pillories to blur the track of his existence ever since they first hid him in this Universe.

One pillory was equivalent to three identities, each one an earth lifetime itself. He had been carefully hidden, transferred, then hidden again, with a new identity each time.

Such precaution was necessary because the Boatman was so good at his job, and because the Boatman was that desperate to find him. His own life depended on it.

Elsewhere, a baby cooed and peed in his diaper.

What an odd feeling, the Boatman thought. This little body is pretty compact with its own drainage system.

The distraction was only momentary. His thoughts quickly returned to 'The Hunt'.

If he didn't find the Grimlot before the trial began, the consequences would be more than severe. They would be catastrophic, not just for a few puny beings, but for entire species. Not to mention for himself!

He wasn't being altruistic in any sense. Basically, the problem had been his own fault. Now, he had to fix it. The only way to do that was to get to the Grimlot first and carry him over the River Styx before the Trial happened. That was the only way he knew how to fix his part in what happened.

Stopping on this planet for his emergency had been a fluke. But, what a stroke of luck!

When he had hidden inside this little human, it had been to explore the planet. Then, when they had been riding along in that cart thing, kind of catching a momentary rest to decide his next move, that's when he smelled the Grimlot standing by the vegetables in the store!

Sheer luck! It had been sheer luck to come across the Grimlot, that was all. After such a long hunt, maybe his fortunes were beginning to turn.

***

Elsewhere, the Grimlot was pacing the floor when his telephone rang.

"Hello?" he questioned. Recognizing the caller, he announced, "I'm in trouble! Big trouble!"

3

How It All Happened

The Old Man had been young once. That's when he first got into trouble . . . on his computer. He would sit at the keyboard and nimbly move his fingers just searching around. Then one day, while on his computer, minding his own business, he had a thought. In the next moment, his life changed forever.

Back then, he had typed into the search bar: "What are the Akashic Records?" and hit "Enter". The answer appeared instantly:

> "According to the mystic Edgar Cayce, the Akashic Records contain ...every thought, word, deed, and intent that has ever occurred at any time in the history of the world..."

The list went on and he quickly skimmed over the words:

> "The Akashic Records contain the history of every soul since the dawn of creation . . . They are mentioned in ancient folklore of past cultures such as Arabs, Assyrians, Phoenicians, Babylonians, Hebrews..."

Everything was recorded in what could be called "God's database." *Yes, and every database can be hacked,* he thought. He knew, then, that he intended to try.

As it turned out, getting in was easy for one with his skills. But the challenge came on another day, while trolling around inside God's database, just hacking for pleasure and enjoying looking into other people's business…he realized with a jolt that he was looking at a weak link in the mainframe! There is was…right in front of him…a doorway into adjusting the files!

He just HAD to hack into it because…well, that's what hackers do. He wanted to see if he could "make a few adjustments". So, he went in and changed the dates of death for a few people. He messed with their life's plans.

At that moment, had he realized the path he was starting down, he might have shut off his computer and gone for coffee. But he didn't, he hadn't, and he'd already had enough coffee for the day. No, instead, he headed down the path of ill-repute . . . Trouble with a capital "T".

Yes, on that day, what the old man did—as a young man – was to hack into the Akashic Records. He messed with God's Database. He found a weak link and used his tremendous skill and talent to access the thoughts, words and deeds of every person who ever lived. Even more astonishing, he discovered he could erase and replace entries with anything he desired! He could cause things to occur that hadn't, and erase results of things that had. He had a way to control Everything. He could control Life itself!

Now, the Hacker hadn't really *meant* any harm when he began playing with recorded events; he only tried a few changes with full intention of putting dates and times back exactly as he had found them. But, then, nature called. By the time he returned from the bathroom, he couldn't remember exactly whose record he was in, or what he had changed. In fact, he forgot just about everything he had done.

What he *thought* he had done was simply change the death dates of a few people who would miss their "ride" with the Boatman on their pre-planned dates and times of expiration. He had only wanted to see what would result. But what he actually did was to start a chain of events that would result in a new course for history in the Universe. He just didn't know it yet.

***

Eventually, when the Boatman came to collect those souls, he couldn't find them at their scheduled places of passing. The first time it happened, he was surprised. The second time, he became suspicious. But the third time, he became angry. He knew this would cause trouble in the connectedness of things and that would *never* sit well with Upper Celestial Management.

It didn't.

An order had gone out to retrieve the Boatman and detain him for Probable Cause/Dereliction of Duty.

Now, the Boatman was sitting in a lonely cell in detention, waiting for what some believed would be a short trial with a foregone conclusion of Guilty. After all, who could not see that several souls had not died on their appointed dates of death? Therefore, somebody was to blame!

Upon arrest, the Boatman tried to explain that he had been at the appointed time and place of each scheduled death, but no one had been there to meet him. However, no one would listen.

In a pre-trial deposition, under oath, he ranted that he absolutely could not find the specific souls who had missed their appointed times of death. What could he do?

But, then, something happened: While awaiting trial, the Boatman was being held behind an invisible retaining wall. One day, he overheard a conversation through the adjoining barrier which was not really soundproof.

Two jail keepers were discussing a recent broadcast about a computer hacker who was bragging that he had hacked into the memory base of the Universe!

The Boatman's attention was on full alert. He adjusted his internal antennae which was among the most powerful ever known. In fact, every cell in his body was wired to listen and hear passing conversations within a wide radius. Therefore, hearing through the invisible retaining wall was mere child's play.

But what he heard, was anything but amusing:

"I tell ya' I heard it as a fact," Blossel said. "A young hacker was telling his story about how he could manipulate people's thoughts. How he could hack into their DNA where memories are stored. He wanted a prize for figuring it all out, so he was telling everybody."

"I he'rd that news," Blossel's companion, Edgert, replied. "In fact, I he'rd he said he could do it again!"

The Boatman stood at full attention! He tuned his inner hearing to listen even more closely.

"In fact, he was sayin' how he done it t'ree times by changing some souls' times of expiration."

The Boatman became tremendously excited. He pressed against the retaining wall to hear every word they were saying.

"Yeah," Blossel continued, "Me mudder he'rd it with her own ears. The hacker said he went into their own personal records, stored within their very DNA, and switched their time and place o' death. He wanted to prove he had hacked into something people could measure."

"Yeah, well, how's that gonna prove anything?" Edgart responded, "Whose gonna know that anyway?"

"Yeah, well," Blossel replied, "To prove his point, he said he RESET their time o' Death for the exact time and date when all three of 'em would croak at the same time."

"And --?" Edgart looked at Blossel with anticipation.

"And, they DID!" Blossel said gleefully. "They all took their last breath at the same time, same day, in three different countries! All looking East, all holdin' a glass of spitzel in their right hands, and they all jumped from atop a five-story building... so as to get people's attention, I guess. And that's exactly what the young hacker said he re-programmed them to do. It made the

Evening Galactic report. I remember it well, 'cause it was me mudder's birt'day."

The Boatman was beside himself! He had to find that hacker! It would prove he was not at fault for missing those death events.

Now, he had a goal: He would find that hacker who would surely do the right thing and testify in The Boatman's favor to get him "off the hook" so to speak, right? This hacker would explain it wasn't the Boatman's fault for not finding those souls at their appointed time of Death. Right?

Wrong! Nothing is as easy as it seems.

Unbeknownst to the Defense Team, one member had it out for the Boatman ever since a loved one had been taken "too early" according to the family. This member had sworn to get even with this figure of Death.

So when the Defense put their star witness, the Hacker, into a celestial Witness Protection Program to keep him safe until a future trial, it would have been a good plan except for one thing: The angry one always knew where the Hacker was being hidden.

Regardless, the Boatman was now aware of the Hacker's existence and started feeling less depressed, like he had been given a reprieve. Finally he had reason to hope . . . reason to believe!

Very slowly, the Boatman began to smile.

4

Other Ideas

But the Old Man had other ideas. Once he realized, as a young grimlot, that nobody was going to give him a reward for hacking into the Akashic Records, he put two-and-two together and knew he had become a "Wanted Man".

He began realizing just what he had done and how important it was for Death to find people at their appointed time, to keep the Universe in a balanced order.

There was one other problem – kind of big-- the Devil had also heard about the hacker and wanted to find him for his own reasons . . . namely his knowledge, ability, and expertise in changing things. So the Devil had sent out a goon squad known as the "Devil's Own" to bring him back alive, or even mostly alive.

Imagine what the Devil could do with the Hacker manipulating God's Database…or better yet, imagine what they *couldn't* do with his special talent.

Think of the ultimate Power it would give the Underworld over humanity . . . over God.

The old man trembled at the thought of what the Underworld could make him do if they found him. He was very aware: They could make him manipulate any thought, word, deed, or activity of anyone on earth, or in history for that matter. They could make anyone say, do, or speak anything desired, all to their own advantage. All because of him and his ability to hack into their life recordings stored within their own DNA.

When God created people, their lives came with a lifetime

warranty of Free Will and a promise that God wouldn't interfere with their choices unless called upon. If the Devil found the Hacker first, would God have to watch as beloved humankind was manipulated by the Underworld because He had promised Free Will with no interference?

The Hacker knew he was now wanted by both Heaven and Hell.

Knowing he would rather be found by heavenly hosts first, he was happy when the Celestial Prosecution Team had approached him about going into Witness Protection, he was on board with their program right away. Because trials and things always take time to get scheduled – not just in celestial terms -- it became eons before the Hacker's trial was actually scheduled to begin. Things just naturally worked that way.

That's why he had been hiding out for so long awaiting the Trial that would set the record straight and remove this enormous burden from his old and stooped shoulders.

That's how he, the young Grimlot, eventually became the Old Man, hiding in a ramshackle house on the planet Earth in the Constellation Cassiopeia, in the Galaxy of the Milky Way, in a far, far corner of the known Universe. This little blue planet was the third one rotating around a nondescript sun. Kind of a pretty, little thing, but still, up close, it was just a hideaway.

But the Grimlot wasn't about to take a chance on being found by the Devil's Own. Nor did he want the Boatman coming to see him personally. Who knew if he might get "other ideas". He wasn't going to hang around to wait and see.

Then, on that recent day when he saw the baby at the supermarket while standing near the vegetable bin, he had recognized the eyes. They weren't real baby eyes.

That's when he knew he had been found . . . and he was terrified.

5

Breaking Out

Life in the Retention Pod was dull and stifling. The Boatman was bored and had almost been wishing the Trial would begin just so he could get some exercise.

But all that changed in a moment once he overheard the news about the hacker. The thought of his new plans brought a smile to his face, the first smile he could remember in over a century.

Today, he looked down the hallway expectantly because it was time to break out of this enclosure.

Ever since he first overheard the guards talking about the hacker, he had begun to plan. He had carefully gone over the coming moments ever since he overheard the guards' talking about the one who had messed with his job . . . and his life.

With new purpose, ever since, he had plotted and planned for a way to escape. Only recently, he had found a way he knew would work, and he knew today would be the day.

He had begun to carefully watch the patterns and procedures of all guards, it hadn't been difficult. He also became familiar with all the electrodes and energies which were keeping him inside the holding pen, and had devised a plan. One thing was for sure – he *would* escape. Then, he would look for the Hacker.

But, how in the Universe, do you find a single soul in an ocean of possibilities. How do you find someone who doesn't want to be found?

With determination, that's what, and the Boatman had plenty

of that.

He heard a noise down the hallway, a familiar one. "Aahh, right on time as usual," he muttered to himself. "That's good, keep on coming."

Two beefy guards with chains crisscrossed over their chests, glided toward his pod. He was the only prisoner, or "detainee" on this wing. The Danger Wing, someone had called it.

Their chains had given him an idea. The Boatman was a master with fundamental forces that controlled everything. He was also very knowledgeable about cause-and-effect. But he excelled at anything to do with magnetism.

Once he realized the guards all wore iron chains as part of their uniform, his plan came easily to mind. Yes, once he began thinking about it, it was very simple, indeed.

As the guards came closer, he recognized both of them as some of the regulars.

"Hello, boys," he called out in a sweetened tone. "I've been expecting you."

The two guards approached their prisoner without care. Why worry? No one had ever escaped the Holding Pen. They knew, beyond doubt, the invisible gate was of a particularly high voltage. In the history of the facility, no one had ever escaped. No one had ever dared.

But the Boatman wasn't like everyone else. His capabilities were far beyond their comprehension.

Today, these guards would make history. Their names would be recorded in the annuls of the jail and studied in future classrooms just by being themselves, their careless, little uncomprehending selves. At last, they reached his holding pen.

"Yo, you called? Food not good enough?

The Boatman kept his head down; his hood falling halfway down his face, covering his eyes.

"Hey, I asked you a question," the bigger of the two burly guards growled at him.

Still, The Boatman didn't reply. Then, he did an unusual thing; he fell down, as if he had fainted, and moaned a terrible moan.

"Call the Medics! Be quick!" said the smaller guard.

"No, wait!" cried out the Boatman. He needed both guards together to make his escape.

"What?! What's wrong with you?!" the big one asked in a loud yet uncertain voice.

"It's my *condition*, I cramp up like this sometimes. I just need to be stood up again. I'll be good then. It's happened before," he said, still keeping his hood over his eyes.

Releasing a lever on the wall, the guards entered the cell. One came close and bent over to check the prone man's face, the other guard stepped next to him and bent as if to lift him. Neither saw it coming.

Grabbing the heavy chains across both men's chests, and with incredible speed, the Boatman moved his hands upward across the chains, in one direction, at supersonic speed, diverting all ions in one direction, magnetizing the chains in the blink of an eye.

Both guards clashed together and were stuck in a frightful way. Neither could move, nor barely breathe. They watched helplessly as the Boatman shook them down for communicators, weapons, and badges, the ones that allowed entry and exit to all the right doors and places. Then, he pressed each one on the side of their necks in just the right spot which made them completely lose consciousness.

Gently, the Boatman lowered them to the ground, stuck together at their chests, and for all intents and purposes, sleeping, but not really. Then, furtively looking around a corner, the Boatman simply walked out.

6

Crash Landing

Looking out a porthole of his flying craft, the Boatman flew swiftly through space. This small vessel was a nice one. He had stolen it from the Flight Bay after overpowering two more guards at the Retention Pod after leaving his cell. With their badges, leaving the facility was relatively easy. Taking a ship was even easier since he was a master at entering and exiting unseen.

He had needed to confiscate a ship because his powers of instant relocation had been rescinded while he was on the run. Celestial Management had simply flipped a switch to ground him. The only instant relocation he could do now would take him directly up to them. But he had somewhere else to go.

Looking over the control panel, he wondered how the gadgets, levers and colorful lights could all look so simple. As a Youngling first studying navigation and the flow of aerodynamics had been confusing until a very kind instructor had explained it in way he could understand. That was good because everyone on his home Expanse had to learn to fly in order to survive.

Now, it seemed effortless; he barely had to think. Almost as if he knew exactly what to push and where to pull in order to blast off. Such intuition was appreciated especially since he didn't want to think of anything but the mission ahead.

He felt wonderful! He had purpose: Finding the Hacker! It would fill every moment of the Boatman's life until he was found. Nor would he fail at something so important. His own future depended on it.

He laughed at how ludicrous that sounded: His 'own future'. But it was true.

Finding the Hacker had given him a new direction! It had been so long since he had a reason for living his life of Death. He guffawed at that inane idea: Life as Death! He liked the sound of his own laughter. Pushing the throttle full force, the small craft smoothly accelerated to warp speed.

***

Sometime later, he again looked out the porthole of his flying craft. The expanse of nothingness spread before him. Yet, it was filled with so much promise. Somewhat relaxed, he began to reminisce.

"I remember one wise man," he spoke out loud, "This man said:

> 'There is nothing hidden that cannot be brought to light. Nothing once known that may become unknown. Nothing is impossible.'

I think his name was Socrates."

The Boatman had taken to speaking out loud. In fact, he had befriended a little blue light on the control board on the upper right side of the deck for lack of a better companion.

Somehow, it felt good to speak aloud and have someone who would listen and not talk back. From time to time, he just needed to talk to someone and, one day, he had simply noticed the little blue light. It had blinked at him.

Now, he talked to it as if the little blue light actually understood him. He had even given it a name: 'Hakor'. It was just a name that popped into his head, so why not?

"I remember this Socrates," he told Hakor, "A nice man... smart! But his people didn't appreciate him. I remember waiting in the garden until he finished drinking that cup... Hemlock, I think they called it. I remember trying to be careful not to disturb his last thoughts. Everything about him seemed gentle. After I took his soul, he seemed pleased with me. That doesn't happen very often."

Hakor, on the control board, just kept shining.

"Ah, I see you agree!," the Boatman nodded. "Good."

What he didn't see was a spiral of smoke that had begun wrapping around his left leg close to the floorboard of the ship. But, as it wafted upward, the Boatman smelled it as it approached his breathing tubes.

"Aghh! What's that?" he cried out. "Hakor, this is unusual. What do you think it means?" Hakor simply remained silent.

In mid-air, the Boatman summoned a navigational chart of this sector of space and scanned anything resembling a possible planet on which to set down.

"Hmm. I remember that one, I've been here before," he said to Hakor and pointed at a beautiful Blue Marble of a planet, the third one rotating around a sun."I think we can make it there and find out what's wrong with this ship."

While the Boatman punched in coordinates to change their direction, Hakor remained silent and said nothing.

"Speak, Hakor, what's on your mind," the Boatman said, then smiled. Maybe it was good he had to land. While he had set down on many planets during his long search, he knew it was never good to be alone too long. He needed to mingle with others.

This time, he would look for a small host body to enter. Co-habiting with one of the species was a quick way to learn about them, their ways and language without being discovered. Contrary to what many believed, Death did not know everything. There was always something to learn.

"Maybe this time, I will find a 'baby', I think they call the little ones. Yes, I'll find one and maybe even catch a nap."

Every species needed time to recharge. That's the way things were made.

The spacecraft entered Earth's atmosphere, and the Boatman began preparing for landing.

Then, Hakor lit up and began blinking. He blinked again, then faster and faster.

"Hakor! What are you trying to say?!"

But, Hakor wouldn't speak as the spacecraft hurtled them toward Earth.

7

Finding the Baby

The spacecraft streaked low across Earth's sky and crashed through a wooded area of the planet. Treetops suffered insult as the flying object clipped their tops, crashing downward into their midst. The vehicle's weight destroyed limbs and branches, finally coming to rest amidst the greenery surrounding a small lake. A waft of smoke crept out from under a casing near the nosecone.

Cautiously, the Boatman opened the hatch and breathed carefully. The air was clean. He detected nothing of danger, or chemicals that would upset his equilibrium.

"Well, let's see where we are," he said to Hakor who had stopped blinking upon impact. The Boatman retrieved a shiny object from on top the control panel and brought up a map into mid-air.

Looks like this is called 'Earth', he mused to himself. "Mmmm, I seem to recall being here a long, long time ago. It's actually so far out from my usual pattern, I should probably find the boatman who travels this domain, but not now, another time. I can't lose focus of my primary mission. Explaining my presence would take too long and probably alert authorities who won't think kindly of my mission. I know they're looking for me, and I must repair the ship as soon as possible. First, however, let me look around."

He looked at the lake, the trees, and far in the distance, a small town. Within a thought he was in its midst, vehicles moving up and down the streets in orderly fashion.

"Not too developed," he said. Having gotten into the habit of talking to Hakor, now, it seemed hard not to speak out loud. *I'll have to remember to think instead of speaking to Hakor though I will miss his quiet company.*

***

As the Boatman began moving toward the small town, a young woman in a parking lot not far away drew his attention. She was lifting a baby out of a car.

Ahhhh, there's my ride. A small human who has not yet developed a strong sense of will power. It should be easy to manipulate for my needs, he thought.

Floating toward them unseen, he quietly entered the baby's small body through its right eye socket. The baby gave a startled cry, but the Boatman was already inside.

"What's the matter sweetheart," the young woman said, cuddling the baby to her chest as she reached for a plastic car seat.

"There, there, we won't be long, then we'll go home for a nap." Carrying her bundles into the store, she selected a grocery cart and settled everything inside the basket before placing the baby and securing him into the seat. Then, she began walking toward the vegetable aisle.

An old man drew her attention. He was standing by the tomatoes. As they drew near, she watched in fascination as the old man looked at her baby, then cried out, falling back against the vegetable display. Tomatoes fell onto the floor and scattered everywhere. The old man, regaining his balance immediately hobbled out of the store.

"My goodness," Marcy said to the baby, "What happened? Well, never mind. Let's just get a few things. We need to be home in time to cook dinner for Dada. You know how angry he gets if dinner is late."

The baby looked up at her and smiled. The Boatman watched through his eyes at the woman. Marcy didn't realize her baby was no longer alone.

8

The Aging

Marcy and the baby reached home just as DaDa did. She was frightened of her husband. He had become abusive and hit her often of late. She had reason to be afraid.

"You're Late!" he yelled at her as they entered the house together. He hadn't offered to help her with any grocery bags, but he did carry the baby in the plastic seat. He really seemed to care for his son.

Then, the words just came flying out of his mouth: "You pig! You nasty piece of shit! You are so ugly no man wants *you*!" The last word was spat out like a bad seed. A deep crease appeared straight across his forehead. His angry words had put a lined mark on his face.

Dada was bored and angry that he hadn't found her in the kitchen. He wanted her to know it. "This is the last time I'm going to tell you to get your big ass moving and make me some dinner!" He deserved dinner on the table when he got home. He was *the man*, wasn't he? It was his due! Everybody knew that. That's how his own father had run the household.

"I'll get it right away," Marcy stammered, scared as usual. "It's just that I worked all day, too, and an accident was…"

"I don't give a damn!" he interrupted her explanation. "Get the damn dinner on the table, *now!*" He emphasized that last word as well.

She needs to know who's boss or I'll clip her, he thought.

Another small crease in his skin appeared above his right

eyebrow. He looked older. Not realizing it, every rough word he spoke to her was marking itself on his face, he was making himself look the way he was treating her. He was becoming an ugly old man.

Bedraggled, Marcy scurried around the kitchen, doing her best to pull a meal together.

Where are those potatoes, she thought. Her hands trembled as she hurried.

"H-how was your day?" she asked. She knew better than not to ask about him, his comfort and his needs. They were always the focus of this family.

"M-m-ph," he grunted. But she had been right to ask. He had been waiting for it. Now he had one less reason to hit her.

***

"Marcy won't have to put up with this much longer," said an invisible entity monitoring the scene from a corner of the room. "She's earned her Goal Experience of Experiencing Abuse as of today and will leave this situation very soon."

The spirit spoke to another entity alongside, one who was Marcy's officially assigned guardian.

"I really hope so, this is hard to watch," the official guardian communicated in Mind Speak. "I've been here since her beginning and she shouldn't be made to suffer more than her Life Contract calls for."

"You've got that right," the monitoring one commented. "The man, however, has a long way to go. He's so deeply Ignorant I wouldn't be surprised if his last lifetime was spent as a rodent. He still has some characteristics of one."

"I don't see any of his guides around, do you?" Marcy's Guide questioned somewhat surprised.

"No, I don't. But, they probably find it hard to watch, too. His soul vibrations are pretty low," the Monitor said. "Hardly any light coming from his soul."

"His face is pretty well-aged with lines of negativity, I see," the guide said. "He even looks older by the minute." Silence.

"Oh, oh, here it comes, Marcy's time to leave," her spirit guide said, pulling closer to watch as Marcy worked by the sink, her back toward her husband.

Looking for something to annoy her, Marcy's husband picked up a fork from the table and jammed it into her back giving a twist as he pushed it. She flinched in pain and surprise.

That was all the excuse he needed. He had wanted one, had been looking for one, so he could give her a swift knock against the side of her head. It always made him feel so…in charge. His large right hand landed on her ear knocking her head into the open cupboard door with a brutal force.

Her head hit the open cupboard door, with loud crack, slicing open the skin above an eyebrow. Spinning, she fell backward onto the center kitchen island then pitched forward onto the floor. Her forward motion was quick, making her head hit very hard against the cold, impersonal tile. Her head bounced once then settled along with the rest of her body sprawled on the floor. Quiet now, she lay at his feet. A trickle of blood made its way slowly out her left ear.

Her Official Guide saw Marcy's spirit rise up from the body.

"Hello, Marcy, I see you are done with this Life Lesson. Welcome to Eternity. We are here to escort you to the next level."

Marcy felt nothing, no pain, no remorse as she looked down at her body lying quietly. Her husband was calling her name, roughly at first, then began using a more quizzical tone.

"Marcy! Marcy? Get up! I didn't mean it! Get up!"

His face was taking on an ashen shade. Two lines etched themselves deeply into his skin at the corner of each eye.

"Marcy! What am I gonna do? What about *dinner*?"

But, Marcy and her two spirit companions, had already left the earth plane.

9

Marcy

Marcy and her two celestial companions had just left the earth plane and were traveling into The Bardo where she would choose whether to go through The Cleansing or return to her life on Earth.

There's no way I'll ever go back to that life, she thought to herself. *I'm done learning about abuse and fear and the results it has on the soul. Besides, I think I've fulfilled my Life Contract for this time. The only thing I hate is leaving my Baby, but I know he is really a mature soul on his own path. His guides will take care of him.*

"That was one of the hardest lessons I've ever had to learn," she sent her thoughts over to her nearest companion in Mindspeak. "Even though I planned that life and lived it, I never want to go through that kind of suffering again."

"You won't have to," Jared, her official guardian, thought back to her. He had accompanied her on her most recent incarnation for its entire course. He had watched her grow into an adult, meet and marry the man from whom she endured countless beatings. He had even tried to help her on many occasions to lessen her pain.

"You have succeeded. You have learned your toughest lesson: How it feels to be afraid and helpless, and not know what to do,"

Jared wanted her to know she was loved.

From her lessons, Marcy had learned to have more compassion

for those who seemed meek and unable to get out of their circumstances. Now, she understood how it felt. Each incarnation was meant to learn and understand all behaviors and emotions. That's what helped a soul become more aware of others and more perfect.

"But it also taught me just how it affects the human spirit being around a negative person. It's like having the air sucked out of one's lungs. I always felt tired and had no real desire to live at all," Marcy was still using MindSpeak. "I had no strength to pull away from that situation, and no one to help me.

"You always had us there, Marcy, and we wanted to help. You didn't always remember to call on us," Jared said. "Even so, your lessons were learned."

"Yes, it was a most difficult path for me. There is one thing I do feel badly about. How will my baby get along?"

"Oh, he has a special path. He will be just fine," Jared told her.

They arrived in The Bardo and were met by a group headed by the tall, elegant entity known as the Serenity.

"Welcome, Marcy, we are so glad you are here, again, and admire all that you have accomplished," Serenity's thoughts were very clear to her.

"After you rest a while, we would like you to choose your next step. There is a new role for which you are perfect. Actually, one you have earned by your positive dedication. Now, that you have learned how negativity impacts a soul, we would like you to consider serving as a guardian angel, one of the highest positions you can be offered at this time. You have earned this most honorable elevation.

"What will I do?" Marcy asked, wondering what would be expected of her, and for whom.

"You will watch over your little one for his lifetime. You will aid him to grow into his future self. He has a very important role to play on earth.

"Do you remember being in the supermarket, just before you crossed over? You were pushing your little boy in a cart near the vegetables. There was an old man by the tomatoes. He looked at your boy and fell back against the bin, scattering vegetables everywhere. Do you remember?"

"Yes, I do." She answered. It happened just a short time before she crossed over. She also remembered thinking her little one was acting different than usual. He seemed more mature, more aware of things around them. She had thought he was just growing up because at nine months of age, he had also just begun to walk which seemed early for his age.

"Not early, Marcy, he was infused with the spirit of a traveler who is very important to us. We need you to become your boy's special guardian. There are plans for his future that must not be derailed."

Serenity was calm with pleasing colors surrounding the area. Everyone seemed relaxed and loving. She felt that All was in Order.

"Yes," Marcy responded. "Yes, I will serve as his guardian angel. Tell me what I must do."

10

Becoming the Boatman

When Marcy and the baby left the supermarket for home to make dinner for DaDa, the Boatman had slipped out of the baby's body to go explore. He hadn't seen what happened to Marcy at the house, and upon his return, didn't know things had completely changed during his brief absence.

He only knew that at this moment, he felt edgy, and needed to relax. As a transporter of souls after death, his job was often mistaken as a scarey thing because, well, isn't everyone afraid of the Unknown?

Because of preoccupation with his upcoming trial, he admittedly hadn't been himself of late. He hadn't been able to do his own job. He didn't realize Marcy was no longer among the living because she hadn't been on his list. He was just one of many boatmen and this wasn't his assigned territory.

In his mind, he traveled back in time. Thinking about just how he had become 'The Boatman':

> *"I don't believe I was born," he said to himself. "I don't remember a mother or father. I just remember...me."*
>
> *In his mind's eye, he remembered himself in front of a fire, a big one. There were shadowed workers piling coal, or logs, or...he gasped!*
>
> *"Are those bodies?" he asked himself, somewhat in horror. He had always had a sensitive side. It was a wonder he had grown into being a boatman at all.*

"Those are bodies!" he whispered to himself drawing nearer. Shadowed figures were tossing bodies into the flames. He looked at the dismal surroundings: Dark corners, dark shadows, no lights, just piles of bodies waiting to be tossed into flames.

Something looked strange: The bodies were empty, no souls filled them.

"Ahh, I remember now, that was boatman school!" It was desensitivity training where one learned how not to care about the suffering of others.

"Yes, that was one hell of a place," he laughed to himself.

As a boatman, even a young one, he had never lost his empathy. He had always been different, and still cared, That's just the way he was. He took the job as boatman because…well, he needed one – a job – it was a better position than anything else he had been offered. Riding in the boat along the River Styx actually could have its pleasant moments.

A cough in the shadows startled him. He looked around. Hmmm. No one. He heard it again.

"Psst, hey, can you help me?" a quiet plea came from an area by a half-hidden pile of rubbish.

"Whose there? Who are you?" he whispered back.

"I need your help," the shadowed figure called back softly. "I've been watching you. I know you care."

He moved closer to the voice and saw a pair of eyes staring back at him from under a cover.

"Who are you?" he asked. Then, ever so slowly, a figure came out from hiding.

In his reverie, the Boatman remembered gasping when he saw her. She was the loveliest creature he had ever seen!

A female covered with a long gray gown with a hood over her head obscuring her face. Her left arm, however, seemed hanging at an odd angle.

"Please help me, I've hurt my arm and I can't tell the others," she whispered. "It would mean the end of everything!" her eyes pleaded with him to understand.

"I've seen you before," she continued. "You're not like the others. I've seen you smile when no one was looking."

The young Boatman was captivated. He hadn't remembered seeing her any time before now.

"Who are you? What are you doing here?"

"I can't tell you," she answered. "But, it's very, very important that you help me and not turn me in to Management. Will you help me? Can I trust you?"

He was too awestruck to think of anything else.

"Of course; what can I do?" he answered.

"Take me to my quarters. I have to lie down and mend my arm."

What an odd thing to say, he thought. But he reached over and helped her out of the corner. As he did so, he felt her smallish frame beneath the gown. She was warm and supple and something about it pleased him very much. He liked the way it made him feel. Usually, no one ever touched each other. It was not permitted, nor desired. But she was different. He felt like smiling, which he did…to himself.

"Come this way so others don't see us."

He led her into the shadows along a path he had traveled many times when he was alone. Which was mostly all the time. He stayed by himself a lot. He never joined the groups. Perhaps he wasn't much like the others.

"What happened to you," he asked.

"I'll tell you later; first, I need to rest," she said. "My room is in the First Quadrant close to the Vortex."

"That's a dangerous area," he responded. "What made you want to stay there?"

He knew she had had a choice. They all did, regarding where they wanted to hang out. No one needed sleep or even food, not in the way humans did. But they had other needs like recharging themselves since the energy that fueled them would eventually run down over the course a work. Their lives were not really divided into day or night. Just time…an eternity of it.

"The Vortex," she said. "I want to be next to the Vortex. It keeps me calm. It's sound is relaxing when I hear it. I like it." She didn't want to tell him the real reason. She didn't trust him that much.

"Well, let's get you there," he said gently. He really liked her…a lot.

Reaching her quarters without incident, made them both feel things would be back to normal soon.

Entering her small room, she pointed to the main rest area and indicated he should wait there. She entered another cubicle that contained a strange long piece of furniture against one wall. It was like nothing he had ever seen…before she pulled a curtain between them.

"I won't be long," she called out. "Just stay here until I return."

As he waited, he heard sounds. They were soft and made a whirring noise. He heard her moan just once. Then nothing. Before long, she emerged from behind the curtain looking refreshed and smiling.

"There, all better," she said showing him both her arms extended. Turning them over, he could see they were both normal. How had she done it? How had she healed herself?

"What did you do? You were in bad shape back there," he looked at her with a questioning expression.

"I have secret powers," she smiled. "But if I tell you, I'd have to kill you," she laughed.

He didn't. How did she do it? he continued to wonder.

From that time on, she remained a mystery, but they continued to notice each other. Without letting anyone else know, they became friends. Something not allowed by Management.

She was in his thoughts throughout the rest of his training. He saw her in the crowd when he graduated, and again when he won his commission to become a boatman, a position to be held for three hundred cycles before moving on.

Those were some of his fondest memories, he realized, coming back to reality.

Briefly, he wondered who was doing his job now that he was on a leave of absence for the trial. He wondered for a moment about her. He couldn't help it; he couldn't forget her.

Looking around, he recognized the house where he left Marcy and the baby. What he didn't recognize was his own situation. It was becoming more precarious by the minute.

11

The Golden Ticket

I can't see or feel the baby or Marcy, yet, the house is full of activity. The Boatman was trying to understand what had happened. *I left them right here. Hmmm, strange. Am I losing my touch?* The Boatman hovered over the trees near the house, watching, realizing their essences were missing.

At curbside, the scene was alive with twirling lights, red and blue from vehicles parked in front. A larger van with rotating red lights was also parked curbside, its back doors wide open. Figures walked from the house to the vehicles and back again.

He watched as an older man was led out the front door, hands behind his back, shackled with iron grips, looking miserable. The Boatman watched him placed into one of the cars. A guard carefully pushed his head down and inside. Then, he watched as a long cart with a white sheet covering a smaller figure was rolled out the front door, down the walk, and pushed into the back of the large vehicle with twirling red lights. There was no soul activity coming from the white sheet, nothing that would speak of Marcy.

"I need to find that baby," he grumbled. A wisp of essence caught his attention. "Aghh, there!"

He saw a car in the distance just turning the corner. It was enough. He had caught the scent; he was on the trail. Instantly, he was in the car where the baby sat in a small plastic seat facing backwards. Another millisecond and he was inside the baby, again.

But something felt different. The baby's emotions were not happy. He could feel a stress, a knowing, an understanding that something was wrong.

"Geez, kid, what happened? Where's your mother?" he said.

Then he heard it, or rather felt it, the baby was talking to him. The baby knew he was inside!

"Mommy, mommy go," the baby communicated.

"Go? Go where, kid," the Boatman asked.

"Up, up," the baby answered.

For the first time, the Boatman could honestly say, he was astonished at what was happening. He had never talked with a live soul in this way before. He was a little shaken. What should he do?

"You'll be ok, kid. Where are we going?" He didn't really expect the baby to know, but he asked anyway. What happened next would never be repeated again in his lifetime.

"Hello, Boatman," the baby's voice had matured, and he was using MindSpeak. "I'm not sure if this was part of my plan or if something is broken," the baby said. "While it's hard to believe, I was assured that I would have a mother and father for my entire existence this time."

Then, he said the most unbelievable thing:

"Would you do me a favor?" the baby asked. "I need to visit the Bardo and check out what's happening. I need to find out why I've just lost a mother that I was approved to have guide me for this lifetime. Will you inhabit this body until I return? I'll be indebted to you in the future."

'Indebted-to-You-in-the-Future' was a Golden Ticket not usually offered by souls. It meant that at some future time, should help be needed, you had a favor due. These promises were priceless.

"Sure, kid," the Boatman answered. "Will do. When do you ----?"

But the baby's soul was already gone. The Boatman was alone in the small body.

"What the ---!" What's going on here? Who is that kid?" Never in his entire existence had the Boatman encountered such confidence, such ability, such bravery!

"I am a fan of this kid!" the Boatman thought, "Hope he isn't gone too long. I think I have an activity going on in my diaper." With that, he chuckled and let go of his – anxiety - for the moment.

He realized he had a Golden Ticket for the future, and planned on using it. Maybe soon.

12

Where Is Everybody?

The Angel's last shift in the Devil's Graveyard was almost over. It had been uneventful this time as she watched a group from the shadows.

Of all the reports she had filed to her real Commander while working undercover in Hell, the only one submitted about herself was the time she had broken her arm and had to mend it using her heavenly powers. That was a long time ago.

What hadn't made it into the report was the soul who rescued her and took her to the dilapidated quarters she called 'home' while serving undercover. He had no place in her report. No need to raise suspicions that would taint her true mission.

Remembering that night, made her think of him. She had never known what to call him. But she had never forgotten his face. There was kindness there, a strength uncommon in many souls she had met while in the Devil's camp. Yet, there was something about him she couldn't forget. In her profession she shouldn't admit it, but she felt…lonely….and missed him.

How could that be? Their encounter had been brief. After that, she had caught glimpses of him around the Devil's camp but they'd never spoken together again. She remembered when he had attained the status of a Boatman. Then, he was gone. That was lifetimes ago.

Professionals in her line of work didn't feel for others, not like that. *There must be something wrong with me,* she thought. Perhaps, it was the strain of nearing the end of her mission here.

She was scheduled to be extracted soon, not soon enough. She was through working this assignment. Working undercover in the Devil's Graveyard had taken its toll. During her entire assignment here, she had uncovered some pretty nasty things. What a full report she would write when she reached her true Home. Yes, she looked forward to some rich rewards in Heaven when she returned there. She could hardly wait.

Her extraction point was set. It would be after her last shift which was almost over. She would return to her quarters and gather whatever she wanted to take. Honestly, there was really nothing to remember this place for, except one thing. It was hidden in her heart: The memory of him. Then she would only have to wait for the extraction team to arrive.

***

Meanwhile, across the Universe, the Boatman was inhabiting a body all by himself for the first time since he could ever remember. Hanging out inside the tiny baby all alone gave him something to think about.

Wow, this kid can barely walk yet I can feel real power in his legs! Being used to traveling at the speed of thought, the Boatman felt this body confinement was a real experience. *I'm just not sure I can take it for too long.*

He watched through the eye sockets as the nice lady kept busy in the kitchen.

With this gravity, it's like being a Neanderthal compared to transporting instantly in the Ether. Golden Ticket, or not, I sure hope the Kid gets back here soon.

The boatman looked up at the kind face caring for him and dribbled on his shirt. The elderly woman laughed.

"There, there, now sweetheart, your mommy's gone to Heaven and your grandpa and I will take care of you for a while. I'm so glad you're still tiny. Maybe you won't feel the pain of her passing. But I will tell you all about her and what a wonderful, kind person she was when you get older. I loved my daughter, and you are a part of her. You are a gift to us."

***

Marcy's spirit was looking at them both from a corner of the ceiling. On her first assignment as her baby's Guardian Angel, she was delighted to see her tiny son and her mom, too. But her feelings weren't quite the same. Now, she was on an official assignment; she knew things were bound to feel different. There was still love in her heart, just a different kind.

Yet, something else seems different, she thought. *Maybe it's because I've never done this guardian role before, but it just doesn't feel like my baby. He doesn't move like I know him. It's as if a stranger is in his body.*

The Boatman simply lay on the bed and cooed.

13

Abducted!

The phone rang, startling the Grimlot. He picked up the receiver with long, gnarled fingers and spoke in a harsh whisper.

"Yeah?"

"Are you alone?"

"What, is this a joke?" he questioned angrily. "I've been alone since I got to this god-forsaken place! What news do you have? Is anyone coming?"

"Patience, my friend," the voice on the other end of the phone line cautioned. "These things take time. Not like you don't have any. Or, maybe you don't, who knows?" the voice chuckled with a cruel timber.

"I don't like jokes. Tell me what you know!"

"Okay. A rescue attempt will be made to extract you in a cubit of time from now. Be ready. I will call back with further instructions. Stay inside. Keep the windows closed...and be sure you shower. Your Grimlot stench is easy to trace."

The phone line went dead. He looked around uneasily.

"Ok, I'll shower. I'm ready to get out of this prison. I've been here too long already."

He walked to the bathroom and turned on the water in the stall. A noise overhead caught his attention. Footsteps on the roof.

"Huh?" he looked at the ceiling. "How could they be here already? I thought I had time."

There was a noise at the window. Bright lights lit the room. He sank into a corner trying to avoid them. A slithering noise came from top of the window closest to him as he pressed deeper into the inner wall.

Smoke began seeping into the room from underneath the front door. Filling the room with ease, it quickly turned into a creature and was upon the Grimlot in seconds, encircling him completely. Rendered helpless in a matter of nanoseconds, the Grimlot watched as two more creatures appeared.

"Wait! Wait!" he cried out. "I know where he is! You don't need me, you want *him*!"

Everything stopped. He felt a reply.

"Who?" his head filled with Mindspeak.

"The Boatman!" he shrieked. "The Boatman is here! I know where he is. *He's* the one you want!"

Shaking in terror, the Grimlot didn't want to go anywhere these creatures were from.

But, he misjudged their reasons.

"Where is he?" one creature questioned.

They had been instructed to bring back this Grimlot, but, if they could bring back TWO desired souls, so much better their reward.

"You'll let me go?" he questioned.

"Sure, we will." the creature answered slyly.

Why should he believe such a one as held him captive? Survival is a funny thing. One hears what they want. Desire colors the thinking.

"Okay, okay! I'll tell you. Just let me go. Take off the pressure!"

Once they loosened the hold, the Grimlot planned to disappear. But the he had no idea who he was dealing with. The Devil's Own had many tricks. One trick was to play with the mind, allowing the victim to believe anything he or she wanted, when none of it was true.

So, while he thought the hold had loosened, truly nothing had moved at all.

When the Grimlot thought he felt the pressure lessen, he tried moving quickly, but it wasn't quick enough. The pressure, again, this time, harder and around his throat.

"Ahggh!" he choked, flailing his arms while turning a slight ashen color as his body lost oxygen. He hadn't counted on a humanoid body needing oxygen every minute. He was unable to free himself as planned.

"Ahggh! Ahggh!" he tried to speak, again. Then he switched to Mindspeak.

"Enough! All right! I will tell you! I swear it by the Devil's Own…" he never finished. The thing that held him squeezed him into unconsciousness. Everything went black.

***

Much later, the Grimlot opened his eyes but saw only space around him. Obviously, no longer on earth, he tried to get his bearings. He looked around and saw that next to him was the baby. It seemed to be asleep, or unconscious. He only knew it wasn't moving.

"Hello, Grimlot," the creature sent him Mindspeak. "We plundered your memory bank. Finding the little human was child's play, so to speak," a noise rumbled out which seemed like laughter. The Grimlot wasn't amused.

"Where are you taking us? What do you want?" His questions

went unanswered.

What did they do to the kid? Why is he lying so still?

The Boatman watched from another layer of existence, not from inside the baby's body. He was watching from a higher level called the Ether that he used from time to time. Other entities had no access to it, but he did.

While they couldn't see him, he still had one big problem: How to keep the baby's body alive when he wasn't actually in it, and neither was its rightful soul owner.

He'd never faced a problem this big. Without a live body, he could kiss his Golden Ticket goodbye.

14

Angel's Choice

The Angel had been waiting for her Extraction when the Capture Team arrived with the Grimlot and the baby. She peered through an opening between two structures.

New arrivals were usually met at an entry point by a crew of the Devil's Own. But, this arrival seemed to have more than the usual number. She could feel an excitement that seemed unnatural. Who were they bringing in?

Finding it hard to see from her hiding place, she dared to edge a little closer but there were still too many in front of her. Did she dare expose herself further just out of curiosity?

Several life spans of undercover duty had made her clever and capable of taking risky chances without detection. She was a professional daredevil of sorts. Why should this time be different? Still, she edged out of her cover just enough to see more clearly, but this time, she was seen!

"Hey, there, you! What's your purpose here? Stand for Discovery!"

The command was imperative. She froze in place. The guard glided over to her and sniffed. She used her cover scent to baffle her identity as she had many times before. The investigator circled around, probing her mental capacity as she put up a mind barrier which was impenetrable to the likes of the Devil's Own. She knew her craft of concealment very well.

"Just reporting for duty," she sent back in Mindspeak.

"Then go where you are supposed to be!" the creature shrieked back at her, unable to detect any smell of deceit.

She glided over to the Entry port and blended in with the last row of workers surrounding the new arrivals.

Then she froze! It was *him!*

He floated above a small body lying prone on a receiving cart. He could not be seen by the others since he was in the Ether layer that only Heavenly creatures and their kind used.

He must be from Heaven! she thought excitedly in her guarded mind language. *I don't think he is supposed to be here. Perhaps, he is on assignment as I am. But this is unnatural, he's caught in a trap.*

Then she noticed the Grimlot at his side. Held by invisible bonds and strangely quiet, the Grimlot was watching his captors from under heavy eyelids and with a scowl on his human face.

At that very moment, her time of decision arrived. From the corner of her sight, she noticed movement in the direction of her extraction point.

They're here! It's time to leave!

Now, it was she who was caught in a trap, one of her own making. She recognized a deep feeling for him entangling her. He was here now, and in trouble.

The group of workers began moving the baby's body and the Grimlot toward a place where new arrivals were processed into the Devil's Graveyard. She silently moved along with them.

Her extraction point faded from view. They would only wait a short time for her to appear. That was the rule. She knew it would not be long before her window of opportunity closed.

Continuing to follow the group, everyone entered the Receiving area of the Devil's Graveyard.

In guarded MindSpeak, she thought: *Perhaps, this feeling of caring is what others have called 'Being Human'. I am beginning to understand why God so loves the world.*

She realized her choice was made. She would stay to help this Boatman who had captured her heart.

The Extraction ship come into view as it lifted off and upward, the one that would have taken her home. With a blip, it vanished from sight.

15

In the Bardo

Marcy's spirit floated above the treeline watching as the police removed her human body from the house on a stretcher, a sheet over it. They placed it into the van. Then, she saw her husband brought out of their house, hands cuffed behind his back, and put into the back seat of a police cruiser. She saw them handover the baby to her own mother standing on the grass.

Not sure what to do next, she began following her mother's car as it drove down the street. It was with great surprise, when she suddenly saw the spirit of her baby rise out of its small body, through the roof of the car and into the Ether layer.

"Wha-a---? Where's he going? It's not his time!" she cried out to no one. Yet, the baby's body was still moving in the car seat in the back seat.

"There's still a spirit inside!" she exclaimed in complete astonishment, unaware of the Boatman's presence. She quickly made a choice.

"I have to follow my baby's spirit!" She thought, leaving the earth plane in pursuit.

Immediately, Marcy and the baby's spirit arrived in the Bardo, an existence between life and final destination. Marcy was careful to stay out of sight. There was more to know before revealing her presence because everything about this situation seemed irregular.

"All of this on my first guardian assignment! What will they think of me?" she lamented, "Incompetent no doubt." But, still, she followed at a safe distance.

Approaching the Bardo's main gate, her mind heard the baby's spirit ask to see the One in Charge. It was urgent, he said.

"On what grounds? You are not on today's list," replied the gatekeeper.

"I require an audience,"

"This is highly irregular!"

"So is my situation," the baby's spirit replied. "I require an audience with the Top Boss."

"Let me see what I can do," the gatekeeper said. "I'll get back to you."

"I'll wait," Baby responded. No one else was in line. Soon, the Serene One appeared and greeted him.

"Why are you here? Your lifetime has barely begun."

"You don't know what's going on?" Baby asked. "I thought you knew everything!" This was concerning.

"Not everything," the Serene One said. "We're on a Need-to-Know schedule. There's been a problem with the Akashic Records being hacked some time ago. Since then, irregularities have occurred in many parts of the Universe. We are looking into the matter."

"Hhmmm," Baby said. "Maybe, I should go above your station; something is definitely out-of-order."

"Now, now, don't be hasty, patience is rewarded, here of all places," the Serene One said, trying a soothing voice. Then, a thought occurred.

"Did you come here alone? Where is your Guardian Angel?"

Marcy knew it was time to make her presence known.
"I'm here," she said in MindSpeak, appearing at Baby's side. "I've been close to him this entire time."

The baby's spirit looked at her. She felt…familiar.

"Do I know you," he asked.

"Yes, my dear; on earth I was in the form of your mother. Now, I have been assigned as your Guardian Angel. The entire situation is hard to explain."

"That's what I have been trying to tell you," the Serene One said. "Since the Hacking Incident, many things have gone astray. It's been, well, a little confusing for many."

"Okay, what I need to know," said Baby, "Is whether my Life Plan is still intact. Am I going to fulfill my destiny and learn my Life Lessons as planned?"

"Of course, you are," the Serene One said. "I'm investigating your case as of this minute." There was a hesitation.

"As you know, WE don't have time here, but that is one expression I picked up from earthlings: 'This minute'. It is so immediate. I love it!"

Marcy and Baby looked at each other and said nothing. They looked back at the shining entity.

"Well, then, you will be shown to a guest area where you can repose while I report this to Higher Authority," the Serene One said. "Please be assured this situation will have a positive outcome. Everything is working toward your highest good."

They were shown to an inner room of great expanse and comfort, while the one in charge returned to a transporter and beamed up to the next level of the Universe.

16

The Agreement

No actual time elapsed before the Serene One returned to the Bardo with a solution unlike any he had ever known before.

In all my time, I have heard many pleas, offers, wranglings, but never once have I experienced the Almighty offering an agreement like this. The head spirit was thinking in Solitude lest anyone pick up a wave of MindSpeak.

I am not sure this Baby's Soul will understand the Enormity of such an offer, I can hardly understand why it was suggested at all. The Serene One neared the Bardo.

Arriving quietly, he summoned Baby. Marcy was not far behind.

"Hello, again," Baby addressed the Serene One. "What have you learned?"

"It is not for you to question! Such Impudence! Who do you think you are?" But, then, he thought to himself in Solitude: He might know he is different or the Almighty would never have offered such a …such a…what do humans call it? –a Deal!

Hhummpph! The Serene One realized at once how uncharacteristic it was to have emotions like this.

It's like feeling threatened, or ---whatever. Maybe a session of reconditioning is needed, a vacation, as humans called it. Whatever is the matter with me? the Enlightened One questioned himself.

I seem unable to control my emotions ,again, as in the old days. Maybe I have overstayed my position. He realized he was feeling desires, again, wanting things! Emotions were so contagious!

It was then he realized, he wanted the same consideration from the Almighty as this one's soul. The Serene One wanted to feel special.

"I hope you understand your situation is one-of-a-kind," he addressed Baby. "The Almighty is giving you an opportunity to fulfill your destiny by issuing a Second Body Sleeve and New Opportunity to begin your Incarnation all over again. New situation, new parents, new life form….do you know how extraordinary this offer is?

The Baby was silent. The he said, "I don't want it."

"WHAT-T-T-T-?!" the Serene One could hardly contain what he was feeling.

"I want my old contract back. It was perfect the way I had it planned," the Baby responded.

"Listen, you little…you little…." No words were found. "Don't be insolent!" the Serene One responded. He felt anything but serene at this moment and recognized the beginning of Anger. This was untenable!

I need help, he thought to himself in Solitude. The colors swirling around his form were becoming all darkened versions of themselves.

". . . Unless, of course, there is a perk involved," the Baby said.

All motion stopped.

". . . a . . . perk?" the Enlightened One questioned.

"Yes, I would like something . . . extra," the Baby suggested.

"What kind of perk?"

"The good kind, of course." A deep Emerald Green glowed all over Baby.

"Like what?"

"Like . . . a Superpower. I want a Superpower thrown in for all my troubles…as compensation for me having to experience this disruption of my Life's Plan after the Contract was made, signed, sealed, and promised!"

Marcy was watching in absolute horror! No one, absolutely no one, ever argued like this.

Everything became quiet. The Enlightened One thought about his conversation with the Almighty. He had been told to make the agreement happen since the disruption of Baby's Life Plan was a "First" occurrence in all of Existence. The Almighty had told him to 'Just make it Right' while acknowledging that all problems started when the Akashic Records were hacked.

"It's getting worse," the Almighty had said. "This hacking problem has got to stop!"

The Serene One's thoughts came back to the present moment.

"All right…on one condition." Was he trying to stall the inevitable?

"What condition?" Baby asked.

"You bring back your first body sleeve in order to make the exchange for your new body sleeve equipped with a Superpower of your choice."

"Alright," Baby said, thinking how unnecessary a second trip back here would be. "But I want this agreement ironclad! Non-negotiable after I return my first body sleeve. Agreed?"

"Agreed," the Serene One regaining control over his emotions again. He summoned an assistant.

"By the way, you should know that your body sleeve has been abducted." the Head Spirit intoned calmly, just as his attendant arrived.

"Show them to the Down-a-vator," the Enlightened One directed.

"Sir? THE Down-a-vator?"

"That's correct. These souls are going straight to Hell."

17

Meanwhile...In Hell

The Boatman and Grimlot were being restrained in a holding pen which had no walls, just an invisible restraining curtain of energy.

"What a hell-of-a-spot we're in," the Grimlot said. "Not to state the obvious. But, look, you are captive because you have to stay with that empty baby's skin to keep it breathing, and I am captive because I possess knowledge of how to change the world. Well, I guess that IS rather important. But I wish I could just forget it all, never have done it."

"Yeah," the Boatman said, "Regrets. I have a few myself."

"You? What could you possibly regret?" the Old Man asked. "Don't you have power over Life and Death?"

"That's what many believe, but, actually. I don't," the Boatman answered. "I follow orders like a delivery man and go where I'm told. If more people knew that, maybe I wouldn't be so feared," he paused. "My secret wish is to be liked, have a friend or two, maybe even find..." dare he say it? "...maybe even find love."

"You? I never would have guessed it," the Old Man said. Something in the Boatman's manner told him he was being sincere. "Then, again, there was this one Grim-lass, way back when..." His voice trailed off.

"Aghh, so...do you think anybody knows we're here?" He said regaining his composure.

"You mean do I think somebody will rescue us? No, I don't think so. It's pretty hopeless," the Boatman answered. "Prepare yourself for an eternity of nothingness. I should know, I've lived it before."

"Pssst!"

They froze.

"Pssst!" It came again from a nearby shadow.

"Who's there? What do you want?" the Boatman called out.

"Not me. It's what *you* want," Angel said, stepping through the force field from out of the shadows. She took in the scene. Two hapless characters bemoaning their fate, not planning a future.

"Remember me?" she asked him, standing in the light of eternal flames outside the room.

"You! I can't believe it! What are you doing here? How did you get in?" he was awash in emotions: Happy to see her, incredulous she should be here, wondering what it all meant. He had never forgotten her.

"Doing here? That's what I want to ask you!" she responded. "I thought you were long gone never to return. I was just leaving here myself, when I saw the Devil's Goon Squad bring you in. Thought I'd stick around to see if I could help. Manipulating the Holding Field was one of my jobs. I know its secrets."

He thought she looked as lovely as the first time he saw her so long ago. Actually, she looked even better than he remembered. A trick of time, perhaps? He didn't know.

She knew. She had always known but had figured it was not in her existence to love another in the way she felt about him. But, now, being with him, again, she knew she never wanted to be anywhere else. Was this a gift from the Almighty? A bonus reward for her long service?

"We'll figure a way to get you out." She said, looking around the quarters. Then, she saw the baby's empty body sleeve. "Why is that here?" she questioned.

"I'm doing a favor for a soul who had to run a…personal errand. He promised me a Golden Ticket if I kept his body warm."

"Must be a special body. That's a pretty high price to pay for a sleeve that others would toss away."

"Yeah, well, I've been inside it and I have to tell you, it is special, in some way," the Boatman said. "Can't quite place it though."

"It's good to see you," the Grimlot broke into the conversation. "Even though I don't know who you are, it's good to see anybody but those devils out there."

"Hello, my name is……"

An explosion interrupted her words, as a fireball hit closeby, sending hot sparks into their area.

"Quick! Follow me!" She unlocked the energy curtain, then motioned them to follow. The Boatman grabbed the baby's body sleeve and followed the Grimlot who was behind Angel. They entered the shadows, gliding down a long hallway the two captives hadn't noticed before.

"Where are we?" the Grimlot whispered.

"It's better you don't know. Clear any thoughts or they will find us through your thinking. Just follow close behind."

The Boatman dragged the body sleeve on the ground. A spark from embers along the pathway lit its foot.

"Watch it," the Grimlot cautioned, "The leg's burning. It's catching on fire!"

Grabbing the sleeve, the Boatman held it close to his face and saw were the foot was burnt. He blew on it, making it glow.

"Combustion," she noted. "When we get to my quarters, I'll take a look at it."

Tucking the body sleeve closer to himself, the Boatman held it like a football. It wasn't breathing any longer, and the color was now a shade of blue.

"Uh, oh," he thought, "Not quite like it looked when the Baby left me to watch it. No matter, it's still my Golden Ticket outta here."

18

The Escape

Marcy and the Baby stepped off the Down-a-Vator into a cool, air-conditioned lobby.

"Are we in the right place?" Marcy asked.

"I have a feeling it's a joke, so when we go through those doors and feel the heat, we'll know we're in Hell," Baby said. "It's a cruel joke. So, yes, we're in the right place."

"Remember, we're here to find The Boatman and when we do, I'll find my body sleeve and we can get outta here," he said.

***

Meanwhile, the Grimlot, Boatman and undercover angel known as "She" were hiding in her old quarters near the edge of the Vortex about to hatch their escape plan.

Outside, a noise captured their attention. Two souls were seen hovering at a corner near the Vortex entrance ramp. They seemed to have knocked over a contraption looking much like a garbage can. Just dumb luck no one heard the commotion since all workers were elsewhere on their workday shifts.

"Why, that looks like Baby!" the Boatman said excitedly. "How is that possible? There's his Guardian Angel, I definitely recognize her!"

"Well, they're going to get captured if they stay outside much longer," She said. "Patrols come by at intervals. I'll go get them."

Before long, She was back with the two lost souls.

"Their explanation is a little hard to believe, even for me," she said. "I'll let them tell you."

"Hey, guys!" Baby greeted them with a wave, sending a flow of energy toward them. "You're just the one we're looking for. Couldn't be better timing!"

The Boatman came close to him. "Do you have my Golden Ticket?"

"Oh, the one I promised if you kept my body sleeve warm? Yeah, that's actually why we're here. We came to get you and my body sleeve to take you Home,"

Something about his explanation didn't feel right to the Boatman.

"And . . .?" he offered expectantly. "What else?" Something just didn't feel right.

"Nothing! Jeesh, why does everything have to be so complicated?" Baby gave a nervous little laugh. "Tell him, Marcy, we just came here to take him Home."

"Where's 'Home?'" the Grimlot asked, "and what do you mean 'him'? Doesn't that include me, too?"

"You? Do you have a Golden Ticket?" Baby asked innocently.

"Golden Ticket?! What are you talking about? Aren't you here to rescue us? Get us outta here?"

The Grimlot was getting upset. He let off a stench to make a human cower, but spirits, not equipped with olfactory glands, were spared from the foul stench.

"Listen, Baby, you can't leave me here! I can help you! I can give you a reason to take me with you!" the Grimlot was glowing a medium shade of red.

"What would that be?" Baby asked.

"You're living a human existence now, but you've lived before and have heaps of Karma built up that you are indebted to pay back in future lifetimes. Everybody does. Well, I can remove that for you! Yes, sweep it away so you don't have to pay back anything. All the bad things you've ever done, I can make like it never happened! You'll be clean as a whistle, yeah, I can do that for you if you just get me outta here!" the Grimlot would have been sweating, if he'd had sweat glands.

"Hmmm, let me think about it . . . okay. Done. You do your magic and I'll do mine," Baby said with an authority beyond his years.

"But, how can I be sure you'll clean out everything?" He remembered one lifetime when he'd acted badly, very, very badly.

"Oh, you'll know," the Grimlot said. "You'll feel differently. Your spirit will glow in a brilliant white energy stream. Everyone will know you're a pure spirit when I'm through with you!"

"Okay, I accept! We'll get you both out of here along with my body sleeve. I gotta have my body sleeve. Is it still breathing?" Baby visually swept the room. "Where is it? You still have it, don't you?" He was getting more excited now.

"Don't worry, I have it in my Supply Room," She said. "It needed a little fix-up. One of its legs got a little burnt. Nothing I couldn't fix. In fact, it's probably ready now," she explained. "I'll go get it."

Anxious to see his body sleeve, the Baby knew he couldn't return without it or he wouldn't be able to select a new one equipped with a superpower as promised.

"I look forward to having all this behind us," Baby said. "Now that we have another passenger, we're gonna have to refigure how we'll all fit in the Escape Pod. I was expecting the Boatman, but now we have this guy," he pointed at the Grimlot, "And I suppose she wants to come along, too," he said pointing as Angel as she came out of the side room holding his old body suit. "How're we gonna do it all?"

"I don't believe that will be a problem," Marcy said. "I've been planning for contingencies and now that things have changed, I'm prepared. Let's talk about how were going to leave."

Their plan was simple: They were going to make a run for it. The Escape Pod had been delivered through the Down-a-vator immediately after their own arrival. It was just big enough for three entities. Now, there were five, and a body sleeve. They planned to squeeze in tightly and hope for the best.

Not much of a plan, but Marcy knew how to maneuver controls and seemed to have an understanding of what needed to be done.

"We'd better leave now while everyone is away from their quarters," Angel said. "Shifts will be over soon and everyone from this sector will be returning for respite."

They looked around and realized there was nothing to gather.

"Let's go," the angel known as "She" said while leading the way out back. A few winding turns later, they saw the Escape Pod straight ahead. Making a run for it, they never heard the whining drone before it landed on top of three of them.

"It's a Grappler!" She shouted. "Don't look up! It beams into your eyes and captures your essence. You won't be able to move! Don't look at it!"

The drone was large with two propellers rotating on each end of a cigar shaped body measuring two feet long. Pulsating lights from the front end were searching close to their eyes.

Baby was the only one not held back. He grabbed the nearest thing he felt and swung it full force, squarely hitting the drone, knocking it off balance. Just enough to let the Grimlot get free and aim a shot directly on one of its propellers with a large chunk of rock he found on the ground.

"It's alerted authorities," She called out again, "Run! Run for the ship! Don't look back!" She was holding the body sleeve and using it like a club to swing at a second drone closing in on top of her.

"MY SLEEVE!" Baby cried out. Marcy was close by.

"I've got this!" She said and began humming and vibrating and turning several shades lighter as the others began disappearing from view. She was using vibrational energy that raised their awareness to a level which made them invisible to lesser beings. And drones were lesser beings, manipulated from a control center by the Devil's Own.

Everyone became transparent as Marcy increased her concentration and energy vibration to a level even she didn't know she possessed.

Under the cloak of invisibility, the Boatman, Grimlot and Marcy made it to the ship. Baby grabbed for his body sleeve from Angel. "Go on, I've got it! Get to the ship!" she cried out, disturbing the vibration and making herself and the limp sleeve visible to the drones again, now aiming directly at her, just as two workers came into view.

"Hey! What are you doing?" one yelled out. He grabbed for the body sleeve and took hold of a leg, pulling it toward himself.

Marcy gave one last push of her mental capacity.

"Hummmmm," she intoned, pulsating inwardly with all her being. Glowing soft white, her energy level vibrated at near maximum. With eyes closed, she thought the purest thoughts possible.

The baby's body sleeve was stretched to capacity and pulled out of the worker's grasp! She threw it upward and Baby caught it.

With a whoop and holler, he yelled in exhilaration, pulling it through the hatch! They had done it! They were free, and he had his precious body sleeve....it was all going to work out!

"Let's celebrate," the Boatman called as the ship picked up speed, propelling out of the bowels of Hell. "Where's She? I want to thank her!"

"Look!" cried Marcy, her nose pressed to the oval window.

Crowding around, they looked where Marcy pointed. The undercover angel was being dragged backwards by the Devil's Goon Squad.

She had been left behind!

19

Angel in Hell

A lot of Earth time had passed since the others had escaped. Angel sat in her holding pen, bored and somewhat dejected.

I shouldn't feel this way, but it hurts to believe you're forgotten, she thought. *In all my service to God, I have never felt the inside of a containment area. Perhaps, this is a good thing so I can know what others feel when they're restrained. Still, I don't believe the Godhead will leave me here forever, I have too much valuable information still to transmit. It just feels like 'forever' right now.*

A noise nearby disturbed her thinking. She floated to the edge of her confined area. A trumpet sounded in the distance, then voices, at first faint, grew louder. Something or someone was coming her way!

A guard from the Goon Squad appeared at her area, looking wide-eyed with excitement.

"He comes! He wants to see you!"

"Who comes?" she asked

"He, King of the Dark Ones, my Lord and Savior!" the guard knelt, preparing for the exalted appearance.

Not my Lord and Savior, she thought. *In all my time here spying, I've never met him. But, then, I've never been discovered before, either.*

A line of guards began appearing, stepping aside and bowing down. A dark figure appeared before her, his identity unmistakable. Beautiful in a way, he was blackened all over as if covered in soot and seemed to smile.

Something about him is actually appealing, she thought. *It is no wonder many are seduced by his desires. If I were not in God's service, I would want to listen to his word*s. She realized her thoughts were on dangerous grounds.

"Hello, there, Bright Eyes," he addressed her in Mindspeak. "I've been told you were trying to leave by our back door, the Vortex. What's your hurry, Doll Face? Not hot enough down here for you? I could turn up the heat, if you'd like." His smile was enchanting.

He's certainly a charmer, she thought. *Better put up my mind shield.*

"Ohh, now, don't be that way," he thought over to her. "You're blocking my best efforts before I've even begun to appeal my case."

She reinforced her mind shield, realizing his seduction was powerful. Of course, it would be, he was God's most beloved angel before falling from grace.

"Why did you leave God?" she sent in a thought-message.

"Ahh, straight to the heart of it; I could use someone direct like you, Sweetheart. Why not give me a chance to tell you about the benefits we offer here."

His thinking was prying into her mind. She resisted with everything she could. But she didn't know just how long she could resist this direct temptation from the Devil, himself.

20

The Super Power

Elsewhere in the Universe, the spirit of the former Baby was picking out a new body sleeve. One equipped with a Superpower as promised.

"I'll take that one," the Baby said, pointing to a long nose hanging on a clothesline-looking gizmo.

"Yes, that one, next to the bulbous nose," He indicated his desired selection.

Because his previous life had been disrupted by the Boatman's arrival, he'd been promised another life, a "do-over" plan with the promise of a Superpower as a perk for all his troubles.

"What's that long line over there?" Baby asked the attendant.

In another department of the body store, was a long line of softly wavering energy streams apparently looking at models of human bodies: all beautifully proportioned. There was a section for male bodies, another for female bodies. Skin tones were different hues of colors: tan, dark, very dark, lighter, light and very light.

"Oh, those are for ones who want a special shape, a perfect model. I've heard it said, *that* body type opens many doors in the physical world and are always in demand. You know the kind: broad shoulders, thin through the hips, small waist, tall, dark and easy-pleasy looking," the sales helper floated around the counter-like structure between the two of them.

"The female shapes are the most desired. Especially, the ones with the large overgrowths on the top part. They don't look geometrically stable to me. And, I've been told that gravity on the earth plane actually distorts them, after a while, pulling everything downward; very likely the cause of falling. I've also heard that some who choose that body type are on their backs a lot. But, what do I know, I've never worn one," the worker turned a pleasing pink tone, obviously an attempt to be friendly.

Looking over at the silhouette of shapes, there was a brief pause.

"Wouldn't I love that athletic shape. What I could do in one of those!" Baby snickered. "But I'd have no time to keep up with all its needs,"

"You really have to wait for one of those, and not everybody has time," the faceless entity laughed at the semblance of its own joke. It's energy field near the top seemed to go up and down a few times.

"You see, in the void, "time" had no meaning," it explained. "There is none!" it jiggled again.

Time or no time, Baby was in a hurry. Once the call had come to assemble a body for Reincarnation, there was a lot to do. One had to have the right shape, look, height, size, and structure.

The most challenging step for body selection to the physical world was designing the body sleeve's face. It could look friendly, fierce, funny, even frightful. After that it would change over time as it became marked by experiences lived in the physical world.

Everyone knows that emotions mark the face with lines of wisdom or whoa depending on the life lived, Baby thought. *I intend to have my superpower's face look full of adventure lines. I can hardly wait!*

"I'll take those nicely-shaped ears," he continued. "And those slightly full lips. I've always liked a pair of those. Do you have any hazel-colored eyes left?"

It was common knowledge that shipments were available until they ran out of stock. Then, you had to take what was left! That's why some people look so ---odd sometimes. They had to choose from leftovers.

Another entity approached them just as Baby was going to ask about the superpower selection.

"I really do wish I had picked out my next body sleeve long before now," it said to the attendant. "I might have waited in line for something decent.

The top part of the attendant's energy field went forward three times in a row in agreement.

"There's only one thing I would stand in line for, one of my guilty pleasures. Do you have any pretty knees? I would LOVE a pair of those; you can do so much with them! People just don't realize what an asset a pair of lovely knees are, until they go through a lifetime without them."

Would you happen to have a pair hidden in the back room, hmmm?" the shopper sent off a pink glow.

The sales blob turned a dark navy blue.

"I didn't think so. Well, that's all for now. I'll be back tomorrow after I re-think the plan for my face. Bye!"

Baby and the attendant were alone again.

"Okay, now for the Big Question," Baby said. "What kind of Superpowers do you have?"

The attendant turned a deep burnt orange and slipped into the back-storage room.

Returning, he showed Baby a case with a lock on it.

"I've been saving this for someone very special," it said, "someone like you." Inside was a very small oblong metallic cylinder.

"Doesn't look like much," Baby said, "What does it do?"

"That's just it," the attendant said, "Whatever you want! It's not confined to just one thing. Whatever you think – happens! You can fly, get big, get small, disappear; most of all, you get strong! Honestly, I've never seen it tested to full capacity. Maybe you'll be the first to try. What da ya think?"

"Hmmm I don't know," Baby said. "How do you put it on?"

"That's just it, you don't!" You swallow it; it becomes part of you forever! How do you like that?" The attendant was positively glowing.

A commotion erupted nearby with such noise they were distracted long enough for a tiny entity they hadn't seen before, enter their area, grab the capsule from its case, and make a run for it.

Baby was quicker and caught the small one, took the capsule and without thinking, popped it into his open orb where a mouth would be.

"Let me go!" the little entity yelled, squirming in his grasp, Then, vanished into thin air.

"Whoa," Baby cried out, "I just wished he'd be gone, and he was! Geez, this capsule thing might be the best Superpower ever! Thanks, I'll keep it! What did you call it?"

"I didn't," the attendant said. "That's for you to do. Tell me know how it goes!"

21

The Years Pass

No Universal time had elapsed since the group had been delivered from Hell while Angel had been captured by the Devil's Own. Yet, in Earth time, ten years had elapsed. Plenty of time for Angel to have fallen to the charms of the Devil trying to seduce her into his own service.

At last, the group was ready to attempt a rescue of Angel from the depths of Hell.

The four of them stood ready: The Boatman, the Grimlot, Baby and Marcy, once mother, now guardian of the Baby in his new body sleeve, all standing ready to descend into Hell and rescue the Undercover Angel who had been trapped when they were rescued. The one who had made their escape possible.

They couldn't imagine all she was enduring, they only knew they were prepared to descend in the Down-a-vator to the depths of the dark place lacking emotions and hope, known as Hell.

Would they find her? What state would she be in? They could not imagine what was ahead for them. They only knew they had to try. Angel must come home.

***

Elsewhere, Angel had waited for them to return. They hadn't come for quite a long time. Finally, she had made a decision. That decision, so long ago, had helped her survive. But she wasn't the same. No one could be the same after living so long in Hell. Now, she was in the Devil's respite chambers. He was reclining on a long platform.

"Do you want more?" she asked the Dark One softly as she rubbed his shoulders.

"Yes, I like how you do it," the Devil replied. "You are special to me. You know that."

Angel was alive. But no one could imagine how she had done it; even Angel couldn't believe it. Her service to God was so long ago, she had felt abandoned and alone. But wanting to survive, she had found a way.

***

The Boatman, however, had never forgotten her. Now, he was behind her rescue attempt.

"We will find her. We have the Hacker able to access Life's Database. We have Baby with his new Superpower. We have a plan. We have each other. What more do we need?"

No one mentioned God.

"What's first," the Baby asked. "Should we get going, or let the Hacker do his magic?"

"Let him hack back to our place of return," the Boatman said. "Try to get us as close to our extraction moment as possible."

The Hacker was busy pointing at colors on the computer screen floating before him. Swiping, pointing, swishing, colors moved by quickly. Then, he stopped.

"There!" he said, pointing at an object on the screen. "That's where we begin. I can manipulate the situation until our present selves overlap our past selves at the exact moment we were being extracted. It's kind of like editing all the time in between as if it never happened. There will be only a slight bump between our old selves and our present ones. I've wiped out all the karma in-between.

"Geez, if I knew that was going to happen, I would have let loose a little," Baby said, smiling.

"Aaa!" remarked the Boatman, "Enough about you; Angel is our concern."

"But Baby is important to us," Grimlot said. "Now, we have the means to grab hold of Angel and pull her into the ship with his Superpower. It will be as if it all happened back then."

The group hustled into the Down-a-vator like a gang going on a road trip. Still, no one spoke of God.

***

The Archangel Gabriel was looking at the group of four preparing to leave.

"Do they think they can do this alone?" Gabriel asked through Mindspeak.

"So many do," the Universal Power answered back. "Most never understand how to pray. They believe that by asking, bargaining, or begging, they are praying. What they don't realize is how to work with the Greater Good: By imagining their desired outcome, giving thanks, and completely feeling what they want to be true, that it eventually becomes so."

Gabriel nodded.

"If they would only realize their gifts as co-creators. But, it takes a highly developed soul to understand functioning on a higher level of existence," the Creator said.

"Yes," Gabriel added. "That's why this Universe is such a good learning system for developing consciousness,"

"How true," the Universal Mind replied. "Everything in its own good time."

The Down-a-vator doors slid silently shut. All riders felt a pulse of downward movement. Anticipation filled everyone as they rode for a second time straight to Hell.

***

Not knowing the group was on their way, Angel was just finishing her day. She spread the scrimshaw cover over the table. Even though she was in a dark place, she had never lost her love of beautiful things.

"That's why I find you arresting," the Devil once said to her. "You remind me of home."

When she had looked at him in a funny way, he reminded her that *his* first home had been in Heaven, too. He had been God's most beloved angel who had begun to believe all the praise he was getting about himself.

"I thought I could do things a better way," he admitted. "The Universal Mind, being ultimately fair, allowed me Free Will to try. That's why I'm here, doing my own thing." Then he roared with laughter. But Angel noted a tinge of sadness in his voice.

By the time she reached her quarters, it was still dark, but almost time for others to begin greeting the workday.

She stayed with the Devil mostly during the dark nights when he didn't have meetings, decisions, planning sessions to keep things running. She was his respite, his comfort, his confidante. Never could she have imagined becoming the Devil's consort. Who would ever have believed?

22

The Rescue (Again)

The Down-a-vator slid to a stop; its doors opened quietly. A cock crowed as if just before dawn, if there was such a thing in Hell. Still, no matter where, schedules are important for things to run smoothly, or there would be chaos.

Now, the gang of four, left the vehicle, stealthily creeping among the shadows to a low, ramshackle cover over a dump of a dwelling.

"Must be home to a very poor soul," Baby said. "I can't imagine living like this."

"This is nothing compared to what I've seen in the Universe on my travels," the Boatman said. "You can't imagine the conditions some souls experience. Sometimes, they gain a higher level of development because of their conditions. No suffering goes to waste."

All were silent now, as they took cover inside the shelter.

"Where to, now?" Baby asked.

"We wait," The Grimlot said. "My calculations say we have a very short duration before the numbers align. Patience, my friend."

Baby stretched out on the floor. Everyone else sat to wait for the Grimlot's signal.

Just then, Angel entered through the back door. Everyone froze seeing each other!

"Angel!" The Boatman cried out.

"What are you doing here?" she yelled in Mindspeak.They all grabbed their heads as her shriek went through them.

"You! We're here for you!"

"No!" she answered "I can't leave! I'm bound by an oath I made to the Devil!"

"What are you talking about? We're here to save you and take you Home!"

"I can't be saved," she cried out in tremendous sorrow. "I gave my soul to save yours, a long time ago!" She collapsed on the floor, her shoulders shaking with emotion she'd never felt before.

"I am bound to the Devil, now; your trip has been for... nothing."

"No, wait! There *is* a way," the Grimlot said. "There is *always* a way!" He turned his back on the group and was moving. No one could see what he was doing. The others just stared, first at him, then at the Boatman, and finally at Angel hunched over in misery. No one said anything. No one knew what else to do.

Time passed.

Then, a peculiar spectacle began to happen. Everyone noticed Angel had become very still. They watched in astonishment as her shoulders stopped shaking and she became quiet. Then fascinated, they watched her form begin to change color from a dull gray to a sparkling bright white. She was almost glowing. Something beautiful had happened. A soft light enshrouded her.

Slowly she lifted her head and looked at everyone. Calm and collected, a smile broke out across her face. The change was completely unbelievable.

"I see everyone is ready," she spoke serenely. "We should get to the Vortex entrance to make our get-away before the workers return for respite."

The Baby, Marcy, and the Boatman looked at each other in astonishment. In a par-second, the Grimlot's attention came back to their gathering.

"Time to go!" he said urgently. "Time to go, now!"

"Let's go," Angel said, leading the way out back. A few winding turns later, they saw the Escape Pod straight ahead. Making a run for it, they didn't hear the whining drone until it landed on top of three of them pinning them to the ground.

"It's a Grappler!" She shouted. "Don't look up! It beams into your eyes and captures your essence. You won't be able to move! Don't look at it!"

Baby was the only one not held down. He grabbed the nearest thing he felt and swung it full force, hitting the drone and knocking it off balance. Just enough to let the Grimlot get free and aim a shot directly at one of its propellers with a large chunk of rock he'd found on the ground. The drone broke into several pieces.

"It's alerted authorities," She called out again, "Run! Run for the ship! Don't look back!"

Baby was busy remembering this scene of so long ago. This was where the Angel had used his body sleeve like a club to take down the second drone closing in on top of her.

But this time, Baby had his Superpower. Quickly he super-stretched a hand outward and grabbed the incoming drone, crushing it with a close of his fist. Marcy was close by.

"I've got this!" She said "Hummmmm," she intoned, pulsating inwardly with all her being. Eyes closed she imagined the purest thoughts possible. Her vibrational energy raised everyone's awareness to a level where they became invisible to lesser beings.

One by one, each began disappearing from view. Marcy increased her energy vibration to an energy level even she didn't know she possessed. Under the cloak of invisibility, the Boatman and Grimlot with Marcy, made it to the ship safely. Baby stayed close to Angel knowing from the past what was about to happen to her. Two workers came into view.

"Hey! What are you doing?" one yelled out.

Now Baby elongated himself, stretching as far out as he could imagine. Then pummeled the workers with speed and accuracy as they tried reaching toward Angel. No match for his super strength and skill, they cowered backward. Picking both up at once, he heaved them as far as he could throw into the distance. Then he took a deep breath and blew, making them tumble end over end down an incline until they reached the bottom and lay still.

With a whoop and holler, he yelled in exhilaration as he followed Angel through the ship's hatch. They had done it! They were free! Angel was safely in the ship with them this time.

It was all going to work out, for real!

"Let's celebrate," the Boatman called from the control deck as the ship propelled out of the bowels of Hell. "Where is She? I want to see her!"

"Right here," Angel said smiling at him.

"What changed?" the Boatman asked. "How did you …"

"I forgave myself," Angel said. "If you all came back for me, then how could I not be worth something?"

The Grimlot sat in his area looking on. Inwardly, he knew that certain things did not need to be revealed, like erasing all the karma she had accumulated during her time in Hell.

Yes, he had hacked the database again, hidden inside himself, when no one was looking.

23

Into the Future

It was a month later, in Earth time, since the rescue of Angel from the bowels of Hell. The Boatman, Grimlot the Hacker, Baby, Marcy and Angel were together in the Bardo recovering from their misadventures. They had just been summoned to give report to a Higher Power.

"What's to become of us, now that we're here?" the Grimlot lamented. "Our scheduled lifetimes are in a shambles; nothing is as it was." He had no idea how to plan the future – if he even had one.

"When I hacked Life's Database, I had a whole future planned. I was going to go into business to change things – for profit, of course. Now, I'm a 'wanted man'," he said aloud, although no one was nearby to hear him."

Marcy and Baby were at an instructional workshop so Baby could learn more about his Superpowers. Since he had swallowed the special capsule, all kinds of things were popping up that he could do. He just had to learn how to control them better.

A strange thing had begun happening between Angel and the Boatman. They were spending more and more time together. The Grimlot had seen them laughing on a number of occasions. He didn't understand it, but at least they were pleasant company.

As for himself, he had no home, no place to go, no one he wanted to spend time with.

"It was better when I had the body of an old man. Going shopping at the store wasn't a bad way to spend time. At least it gave me something to do."

Then he wondered: *What would I really like to do?* Travel more, came to mind. *But first, I've got to get out of my legal bind. What am I going to do?*

Angel and the Boatman had also been thinking about the future. A long time ago, they had first noticed each other when he had been starting out as the Boatman, and she had been on undercover assignment. Now, their friendship was blossoming and neither wanted to be alone again.

"Why don't we go visit the Grimlot," the Boatman said. "I have an idea. It's far out, but it just might be our solution." Angel was intrigued. She had been given time off because of her lengthy assignment in Hell, and planned to take full advantage of it.

They found the Grimlot in a quiet place. The Bardo had many such spaces, mostly spread out and used for reflection on past lives. These quiet areas were restful with peaceful surroundings.

"My friend," the Boatman greeted him.

"Hello?" the Grimlot wasn't exactly easy with the term "friend" as yet.

"Angel and I have been thinking about 'an arrangement'. We'd like to know what you think."

Angel turned slightly rose-tinged since she didn't know exactly what he was talking about.

As you know," the Boatman started. "Angel is on sabbatical, and you and I are in legal trouble until we clear things up with the Universal Court. That is, if they can find us. Now, I've been thinking that you have caused my troubles, and I can help you out of yours, if we make this arrangement."

The Grimlot was intrigued.

"In all my time of being a Boatman, no one has ever looked me in the face. So, my proposal is for you to take my position where you will never be discovered since no one looks into the face of Death…," he hesitated. The Grimlot was still listening.

"And I could go away with Angel to a far, far place where we could do some good for other souls who need to be loved. That is my dream."

Turning to Angel, he added, "That is, if you'll have me as your true companion."

No one said a word, not in Mindspeak, nor out loud. Then, slowly, Angel turned a brilliant white and sent out a message: "Yes, I accept."

The Grimlot sent out a message of his own: "Yes, I accept."

The Boatman was speechless. He had never felt so happy in his entire existence.

Close by, the Archangel Gabriel was watching, and sent a message to the Universal Mind.

"They've all accepted the deals. Now what?"

"Now, they will live their lives with Free Will as has always been allowed. They will learn from their desired lessons and continue to develop their souls from all their opportunities," the Universal Mind shown as a brilliant white light.

"One thing they've gotten right: It is Love that matters most of all."

***

Not 'The End'...

24

The Message

The Dark Lord locked the door of his den, then sat heavily into his Executive chair. It was positioned behind a massive, ornate desk of unusual material, rather effervescent. He looked as if the weight of the world was on his shoulders. Downcast, he formed the darkest thoughts possible.

So close. I was so close. There won't be another chance like that in a million years. Maybe never.

His communicator buzzed. A message was coming in. Glancing inwardly at the hologram in his head, the message entered his thoughts.

It was from…*Him.*

The Dark Executive smiled, a devilish grin. His tail swished back and forth in pleasure. The view inside his head was of a heavenly scene. Words appeared mid-brain; it was the same message he had received long ago…even before the idea of Man had been conceived.

The first time the Dark One had received this same message, he had ignored it. Now, he was receiving it…again. This time he welcomed the communication. His beliefs had softened from that time so long ago.

"I look forward to you coming home."

The message glowed in gold letters.

"It has been too long...even for you." The message ended there.

Always brief and to the point, the Executive thought. *That's the way I remember Him to be. Even more so, He is right...the way it has always been.*

The Dark Lord answered with a message in his own mind. Instantly, his words were delivered as soon as they formed in his head.

"I know you will forgive me, because that's who You are. The problem is mine, all mine. I just can't pay back the crush of karma that I have accumulated over the eons. This situation with the Grimlot was my one chance to return to you by erasing all penalties and debt I have accrued. Without the Grimlot erasing my karma, as he could have done, my return to You will have to wait...perhaps, another time. But you know . . . I miss you, God," the Devil said, "I miss you very much."

A last message came through. It simply said:

"I miss you, too."

Meet the Author

Born at an early age, Paula F. Howard has been a writer since childhood. A returned Peace Corps Volunteer, she served in South America as a nurse in one of the first groups to go overseas.

Throughout her various careers, she has loved writing the most. As a journalist, news editor, and photographer for newspapers and publications, she has been recognized by numerous organizations for her professional skills. As a public relations/marketing executive in business, she enjoyed producing large special events. As a registered nurse, she watched in awe at the human condition and all the various forms in which it manifests.

Her greatest achievement, however, was raising three children to adulthood, and is grateful for every precious moment with them.

"Of all I have learned, the most important is that we are as human candles, here to light the way for each other."

Besides "The Angel and The Boatman", she has authored "The Hidden Pricetag" , "Memories Today" and "The Power of One" an inspirational calendar about the power we each have inside ourselves. All are available on Amazon.com. She has also created the online resource for authors and writers called TheWritersMall.com

A former radio DJ while living in Puerto Rico, she is currently recording audiobooks through ACX.com

Available for speaking engagements, she can be reached at Paula@ PaulaHoward.com.

Here is an exerpt from The Hidden Pricetag
Available now on Amazon.com and at TheWritersMall.com

The Hidden Pricetag

Everything has a cost
Are you willing to pay
the price?

How the world REALLY works
A metaphysical novella by p.f.howard

THE HIDDEN PRICETAG

Anything you want…ANYTHING…prices vary.The sign was unmistakable. It hung by two hinges above a plain door over a cobblestone street.

The sign was dull red with black letters. The word "ANYTHING" larger than the others and on its own line.

In the window, stacked pillars covered with silky brown material displayed several items of varying sizes. A large oval platter in the middle of the display had several delicious-looking candies, some with nuts, others with fruits: each one had a price tag attached facing down.

I pushed open the door and entered the shop. There were no aromas. No one was there. Walking over to the window, I reached inward. Touching one of the tags on a particularly delicious-looking offering. I turned it over and read: "Rich beyond your wildest dreams."

I dropped the tag and stepped backwards.

"May I help you?" a voice came from behind me. "Do you want something? Prices vary," the voice said as I slowly turned around. I was looking at…. myself…as if in a mirror… but it wasn't me. The real me stood with my back to the outside door. The strange "me" stood between the counter and a doorway behind her from where she…("I"?) …. had just entered the room.

"Can I help you?" she asked, while walking around the counter to stare me full in the face. "Do you see anything you would like?" She smiled and waited.

"I-I-I don't know," I stammered. (Was I really talking to myself?)

"Well, take your time. There's a lot to choose from. It can be overwhelming," She had a Mona Lisa smile...I couldn't quite figure what she was thinking.

"Perhaps, if you would think back into your past...was there anything you wanted, and didn't get? Anything at all... our prices vary." Her voice was hollow of emotion. Suddenly, I felt cold and wanted to leave, but she now stood between me and the door.

"I don't think you want to leave just yet...you've only just begun your selection." Something about her was frightening...yet comforting at the same time.

"You know," I began, "I thought there was something, but now I'm not sure...I may actually have everything I need." My mind raced. How could I get around her and out the door? Who knew I had come here? Jason was the only one, and no doubt, by now, he wouldn't care. I had yelled at him that I wanted more! I was probably the last person he wanted to see ...maybe ever.

Turning back to the window, I hoped she would think I was making a selection, then I would bolt for the door.

But she anticipated my move.

"That's okay, dearie, everyone's nervous the first time they make a selection. It's much easier if you close your eyes and pick one. That is, if nothing comes to mind that you really want ... remember, prices vary."

I felt heavy, unable to move. How had I gotten into this predicament? I moved toward the door, hoping to reach it before she did...but suddenly, she was there! The room spun, and I felt dizzy...I was falling. I gave into the darkness and hit the floor.

Slowly, my eyes opened to see a pair of shoes ...with feet in them. Looking upward, I saw... Me, again. It hadn't been a dream.

"Now then," she said, "Are you ready to begin?"

I didn't know what to say. It felt like I was thinking what she was saying. Words tumbled around in my mind. Slowly, I stood up, checking that everything was alright. I looked at the window again and noticed a certain bonbon that seemed more inviting than the rest.

Reaching into the display, I turned the tag over: "Rich beyond your wildest dreams!" Then, I noticed the price: "A loved one must die."

"What is this?!" I cried out. "Who are you?" I screamed at her. "Let me out of here!"

Reaching for the door, the handle came off in my hand!

I turned…as she approached me…and walked right into my chest, melding into my body!

Screaming out loud…I heard only a faint echo return…. "Now, let's get started," it whispered to me.

2
THE PHONE CALL

Just a little further, I thought to myself.

I left it somewhere…ahh, there! Heading toward the distinctive back end of a dark blue Prius among a line of cars, the keyless entry fob felt hard in my hand.

For just a moment, a funny feeling thrilled in my chest…like a flutter. I couldn't remember where I was coming from, but I'd forgotten such things before. What mattered more was where I headed now.

Home to my husband, Jason…to make up for this morning's quarrel; maybe I would make his favorite dinner. I could shop on the way home.

The flutter, again. This time, it felt stronger. Strange feeling, almost like something was going on inside my chest.

"I'd better have that checked out," I said aloud. Strange feeling…kind of eerie.

The supermarket at Third and Main Street was crowded as I went through the door. It took only moments to find ingredients I needed among the aisles. Checking out, I headed back to my car. Red and blue flashing lights at the corner caught my eye.

There were lots of lights…and police cars… and people gathering quickly. I craned my neck to see better, but couldn't, as I entered the driver's side.

"Always something," I thought, starting the engine. "I'll drive out the back and avoid it all."

Arriving home, everything looked peaceful. Carrying grocery bags, I entered the side door into our kitchen when two things happened at once: I noticed a beautiful bouquet of gorgeous red roses on the table, wrapped in parchment paper; and I heard the phone ringing loudly...and long. We still had a land line in the kitchen, even hanging on the wall. How retro, but for us, it worked.

Reaching for the receiver, I answered, "Hello?"

"Is this Mrs. Seaver? Angela Seaver?" the voice was official, hard and unemotional.

"Yes, it is."

"I regret to inform you that Jason Seaver has had an accident. Can you come to Parkland Hospital? We need to talk with you."

Oh, my god, Jason!

"Is he alright? Is he hurt?" Of course, he's hurt, I thought, He's in the hospital.

"Yes, of course. I'll come right away. You mean to the Emergency Room? I'll be right there."

Grabbing my keys, again, I hurried back to the car. Damn. There's that flutter in my chest again.

Entering the sliding emergency room doors, I looked for someone to talk to. A receptionist caught my eye. I hurried over. She politely answered questions and motioned to a side door; I quickly entered.

Finding the bay where Jason lay was easy. Several policemen were visible standing by the blue curtains. It was strangely quiet, no hustle, no activity near them at all.

Looking inside, I saw Jason lying quietly on a cart, his eyes closed...looking peaceful and... quite dead.

"Oh, my god!! Noooo!" I cried out and buried my head on his chest. It was cold...hard.

 Sobs wracked my shoulders. His body gave slightly with my weight upon it. Tears streamed down my face as I looked at him, thinking of our last words, so harsh, so unforgiving, so...unnecessary!

"Oh, my Darling, please forgive me, I love you so much!"

My grief turned to quiet sobbing. A nurse appeared with a glass of water. The policemen were out of view, giving me final moments of privacy. Jason lay there, quiet and reposed.

A memory tickled my mind. Something about a price tag…but the memory was just out of reach. It wouldn't reveal itself. The flutter in my chest came again… then, stopped. I sat there and cried.

Jason's dark hair was matted to his forehead. There was a red bruise on his right temple, but no other sign of trauma on his face, nothing above the sheets. I noticed, though, that his head appeared to be lying at an odd angle.

"Mrs. Seaver?" A middle-aged doctor stood by the curtain, holding it aside. He quietly entered.

"I'm Dr. Randall." His name was embroidered on his white lab coat.

"I am sorry to tell you that your husband was in a car accident this afternoon by Third and Main. Apparently, he tried to swerve out of the way of something, or someone, and ran into a light pole. He hit his head on the steering wheel at such an angle that his neck snapped. He died instantly…didn't suffer at all."

My head felt full, as emotions played in my mind: Upset, anger, disbelief, love lost, relief that he hadn't suffered. I was the one suffering now.

Dr. Randall kindly let me ask all the questions that came to mind, knowing I was processing a deep grief. But he couldn't answer the most important one: Why? Jason was such a careful driver, not one to make quick movements…or judgements…not at all. But, then, why does anything happen? Life, I suppose… life intervenes when you've made your other plans, I thought.

Something vaguely stirred inside me. The flutter again? No, something else. Something deeper, like the thought of… a smile.

The curtain was pushed aside, again. This time a tall man in a dark, gray suit stepped inside.

"Mrs. Seaver? I'm Detective Bradley of the city Police Department. May I have a moment?" I nodded. My mouth trembled a little.

"We're so sorry for your loss." He took a notebook out of his pocket. "The reason we're investigating is because of the way it happened."

His look was direct and full of intent. "There were no skid marks on the street, and his head hit the steering wheel before the air bags deployed."

He stopped and looked hard into my face. "It's real strange the way it all happened," He took a breath.

"Was anyone after your husband?" The question hung in the air. "Was there anyone he might have been trying to stay away from?" He waited for me to answer, but I had nothing to say.

"Could he have been having…an affair?"

It was late when I returned home. My thoughts still on the questions, the paperwork, the phone calls and all details of bringing someone's life neatly to an end. I felt exhausted.

Out of the corner of my eye, I saw the beautiful red roses still on the table. A last gift from Jason. Oh, my darling, I miss you so!

Picking up the bouquet, I unwrapped the flowers carefully, never noticing a small paper as it fluttered to the floor.

Arranging stems in a deep vase of water, I positioned the beautiful arrangement in the center of the table. Then, pouring a glass of wine, sat down to let everything settle in.

"That's it, dearie," a voice in my head seemed to say.

What was that? A thought? It didn't seem like my own.

"Now, look down."

The small paper was barely visible, just a corner of it sticking out from under the cabinet's edge. Bending down, I could easily see it was…a lottery ticket.

"Yes, my sweet, and now…" the voice inside me whispered, "…it's time to play!"

IF YOU'VE ENJOYED THIS EXCERPT OF 'THE HIDDEN PRICETAG", YOU CAN ORDER THE FULL COPY ON AMAZON.COM

Made in the USA
Columbia, SC
27 January 2022

54660744R00057